The
BECKET
LIST

A Blackberry Farm Story

The
BECKET
LIST

A Blackberry Farm Story

Adele Griffin
pictures by LeUyen Pham

Algonquin Young Readers 2019

Published by
Algonquin Young Readers
an imprint of Algonquin Books of Chapel Hill
Post Office Box 2225
Chapel Hill, North Carolina 27515-2225

a division of
Workman Publishing
225 Varick Street
New York, New York 10014

LIBRARY OF CONGRESS CATALOGING-IN-PUBLICATION DATA

Names: Griffin, Adele, author.
Title: The Becket List : a Blackberry Farm story / Adele Griffin.
Description: First edition. | Chapel Hill, North Carolina :
Algonquin Young Readers, 2019. | Summary: When New York City
native Becket Branch moves to the country with her family to help run her
grandmother's farm and store, she finds that new friends, hostile chickens,
sour lemonade and mischief are only the beginnings of her new life.
Identifiers: LCCN 2018027330 | ISBN 9781616207908 (hardcover : alk. paper)
Subjects: | CYAC: Country life—Fiction. | Moving, Household—Fiction.
Classification: LCC PZ7.G881325 Bl 2019 | DDC [Fic]—dc23
LC record available at https://lccn.loc.gov/2018027330

10 9 8 7 6 5 4 3 2 1
First Edition

For Robert, Christine, and Greyson Watson

HOW TO BE
A COUNTRY KID

1. Goodbye, City!

2.

3.

4.

5.

6.

7.

8.

9.

10.

CHAPTER 1

Goodbye, City!

TODAY WE'RE MOVING TO BLACKBERRY FARM. MY PARENTS are taking over the Old Post Road Animal Clinic, and we'll all help Gran run Branch's Farm Store.

Mom and Dad said we couldn't go until everything clicked into place.

Like my big sister, Caroline, had to finish sixth grade. And my twin brother, Nicholas, and I had to finish third grade.

Plus we had to buy a used car.

Also we needed to pack up all our stuff. It's harder than you might think, since Nicholas keeps unpacking it. He's not as ready to move as I am.

Moving to the country always sounded more like a story than a plan. Caroline, Nicholas, and I have only ever known city living. Dad grew up on Blackberry Farm, but he and Mom have been city vets for as long as I can remember. They had side-by-side offices down the street at Urban Hope Animal Shelter, where they took care of mostly cats and dogs.

But now—CLICK—everything is changing. Moving Day is finally here!

"Goodbye, Branch family apartment," I say as I hop out of my sleeping bag. "Goodbye, *roo-koo wak-wak* pigeon sounds outside my bedroom window. Goodbye, buildings and water towers."

Caroline rolls over in her bag. "Rebecca, hush. It's Sunday. Everyone sleeps in on Sunday."

"Not on *moving day* Sunday!"

Caroline flips her pillow over her head. Last week, I heard her say to her best friend, Annabelle Fair, that the only thing she's looking forward to about the country is not having to share a room with me. So I'm pretending I'm really excited to be getting my own room, too. But secretly it's the part of the move that I don't want to think about. Caroline and I grew up sharing a room. I can't imagine how it'll feel not to have her with me at night for ghost stories or burping contests or thunderstorms.

I put on my glasses and head to the bathroom.

In the mirror, I brush my teeth (big, square, space in the middle), my hair (brownish-wavish-shortish) and check in with my nose freckle (still here).

"Goodbye, sink. Goodbye, squeaky-flush toilet."

Even though I've lived here

my whole life, I never saw our apartment empty. Now I see scratches on the floor where tables and chairs used to be. I see marks on the walls where our pictures used to hang.

In the kitchen, Mom hands me a paper bag. "From Sugarman's Deli," she says. "One last egg-and-cheese on a roll."

"Goodbye, Sugarman's Deli!"

"Don't make me go!" Nicholas wails first thing when he stumbles out to the kitchen. It was also the final thing he wailed before bed last night. His face is blotchy. Whatever my twin brother is feeling, he wants to let you in on it. "Please, please don't force me to live in the country with mice and skunks!"

"Eat," says Mom. She gives him his egg-and-cheese. "Everything feels worse on an empty stomach."

But it's not just Nicholas's empty stomach talking. All of his parts are upset.

"Guess what? I had a really good idea," I announce. "I made a list for how to be a country kid."

"That's fun, Rebecca." Mom smiles. "Show it to Nicholas, to get him in the spirit!"

Nicholas sends me a look that says: Don't mess with my spirit.

There's only one thing on my Country Kid List so far, but Nicholas doesn't need to know that. He doesn't want to see the bright side of anything today. Right now he wants to be deep in his gloom.

"The first thing on my list is: Goodbye, City!" I say. "That means saying goodbye to the city. Starting with our apartment. Goodbye, crack in the wall that looks like a starfish! Goodbye, freezer where my tongue got stuck!"

"Speaking of goodbye, I'm packing last odds and ends into this brown box," says Mom as she sets it down.

"I'm unpacking my pillow," says Nicholas, reaching in. "I need to hold it."

"Goodbye, radiator that hisses like a snake! Goodbye, height-measure marks in the doorway!" I rub the mark from when I turned five years old. Wow, I was such a shrimp. But I learned to swim and I aced kindergarten that year, too.

"Goodbye, brave shrimp," I whisper to that old me.

Mom, Caroline, and I are taking the train to the farm. Dad's driving Nicholas and our dog, Mr. Fancypants, since there's not enough room for us all in the car. The back seat is stuffed with everything the moving truck hasn't loaded. Like sleeping bags and Mr. Fancypants's special firm-surface arthritis bed and Nicholas's cello, Clive.

Mr. Fancypants just snuffles around. He's confused about the

6

empty apartment. It's the only place he's ever lived. He is mostly blind and he keeps bumping into the walls. "Take it easy, ole boy," I tell him, scratching behind his ears. "You'll be happy to retire to the country. That's what all oldsters like to do, unless they go to Florida, like Neeny and Gamps." Neeny and Gamps are our grandparents on Mom's side. We've visited them in Florida many times. Florida is the orange juice and old people state.

When it's time to leave, I pick up my gold glitter suitcase. Then I kiss the door. "Goodbye, front door. Goodbye, Mrs. Wetters in 8E who doesn't give out Halloween candy. Goodbye to the fantastic Fairs. Goodbye, lumpy hall carpet. Goodbye, menthol-cough-drops hall smell."

"Okay, Rebecca," says Mom. "I think that's enough goodbyes."

But I don't want to forget anything. Goodbye only happens once.

"Goodbye for good, city," Dad says from the door as we head to the elevator.

Then I stop.

"Wait." My heart is suddenly pounding. "This is the last time I'll ever walk out the door of 8D." I turn around to take a picture for my heart. Dad stands in the doorframe, finishing his egg-and-cheese. Nicholas is holding his pillow in front of him like a shield.

My twin brother's eyes are big and dark and owlish. He's worried enough for the both of us. If I look scared, he'll get worse.

"Goodbye to ever getting stuck in this elevator again!" I say in my braver-twin voice. Nicholas got stuck in our elevator once when he was six years old. Even though he was trapped for only fifteen minutes, he still talks about it.

"See ya later, elevator!" he shouts.

Once we're out on the street, I breathe better. "Goodbye, R-train subway stop. Goodbye, dry cleaners. Goodbye, smelly garbage truck."

"Goodbye, gingko trees in June," says Caroline.

"Caroline, no!" I shake my head. "That's one thing you don't have to say goodbye to. We'll see tons of trees in the country!"

"These are our street trees," says Caroline. "They're like our neighbors."

"GOODBYE, NEIGHBOR TREES!" I yell to them all as we walk to the subway that will take us to the train station.

Outside the subway, I spy a billboard for Country Goods Farm Markets. It's a photograph of lettuce and tomatoes and ears of corn. In the sunshiny background, a girl and her big, gorgeous, floppy-eared dog are running down a hill.

"Look!" I shout. Mom barely looks. But I know this billboard is a sign of my new life, starring me running around in the sunshine with my very own dog—*not* fat old Mr. Fancypants who only likes Nicholas. A big, beautiful, floppy-eared country dog has been my wish since I don't even know how long.

The subway is packed. Across from me sits a guy with hair on his hands. The rest of him looks normal, then— crazy hairy hands!

Like a wolf-man!

"Um, Caroline," I whisper. Then I whisper louder, "Caroline Caroline Caroline Caroline Caroline *Caroline* CAROLINE. That man across from us is a WEREWOLF!"

"Rebecca!" Mom frowns and puts a finger to her lips.

The man's shaggy eyebrows lift. Caroline pinches my arm. But when we get to the train station, Mom buys me a bag of roasted pumpkin seeds anyway (my favorite), along with Caroline's favorite, Frootberry Swizzlers.

"He might have been part werewolf," Mom admits. One thing about Mom—she sees all sides.

We buy our tickets and walk out to the platform. I sit down and unzip my suitcase where I keep my best stuff. Besides my notebook and two cheese sticks, I packed my five hammies, three hamblings (hamblings are baby hammies), plus the tiny pirate hat that goes on my favorite hambling, Pirate Punkin.

Hammies and hamblings are the next greatest thing to having a suitcase full of real hamsters. But these cuties run on batteries and can do tricks like roll over. As soon as I take them out, they all start peeping and hopping.

Mom looks down. "Rebecca, switch off your toys! And get up from the floor, it's so dirty!"

"Hammies and hamblings don't have an off button, remember? Here, hammy hammies! Hop back in your suitcase, my little furry sweeties!"

"Sometimes I wish *you* had an off button, my sweetie," says Mom. "I know . . . maybe it's here?"

I move to cup my hand over my nose freckle—but I'm not quick enough. Mom leans down and presses it just at the same time the bell starts ringing.

The train is coming in!

"Goodbye, every last thing in the city!" I call out. "Goodbye! All aboard!"

CHAPTER 2

Becky? Reb? Becca?

"LET'S SIT IN THE MIDDLE," SUGGESTS CAROLINE.

"No, let's sit in the front car near the engine," I say. But a family with a crying baby got there first.

"Too loud!" I decide. "Let's sit in the last car and be the caboose."

There's nobody in the last car. "This feels too quiet for an adventure."

"Okay, Rebecca, I'm taking you off seat choosing," says Mom. "The next three free seats are ours." We find them smack in the middle of the train.

13

Caroline smirks. "You should listen to your big sis."

"The middle of the middle was my next suggestion," I tell her.

The train moves slowly out of the tunnel, traveling uptown. Soon tall buildings turn into short buildings, and then short buildings turn into fields.

Once we're settled, I switch places with Mom. I like to stare out the window, watching the world go by.

"My whole life, I've been a city kid," says Caroline. "Starting today, I'm a country bumpkin."

"I'll never be a bumpkin. Besides, I like changes," I say. "In fact, from now on, please call me by my new cool country nickname. It's on my list." This is not totally true, since I just thought up my nickname a second ago.

"What is it?" Caroline looks at me like she's trying to guess it from my face. "Becky? Reb? Becca?"

"Becket!" I shout.

Mom sits back, crosses her arms, and says, "Oh."

"Becket? That sounds like a boy," says Caroline.

"Rebecca doesn't fit me," I say. I'd started thinking about this last year, when I saw my name on my goody bag after my friend Sophia's ice-dancing birthday party. The *Rebecca* was silver and curly. The last *a* swirled into a very long ribbon across the bag, like *a* was a sound that could go on forever. That was when I started wanting to give my name a haircut. I'm not a curls and ribbons kid.

Caroline's face is making my new, trim name shrivel inside me. Mom has been quiet too long. Nobody likes it? Why not?

Caroline offers me a Frootberry Swizzler. I shake my head no.

She chews on hers for a while. Then she points her Swizzler at me like it's a magic wand. "You know what? Becket is more you. Sometimes when a person has a new idea, it takes the rest of us a while to catch on."

"That's true, Caroline," says Mom. "Let's give Becket a try."

I feel my new name blooming inside me again.

Mom goes back to her book. Caroline plays on her phone. Out the window is a blur of moving trees.

"How about some family talk time," I say. "Mom, that looks like a good book about . . ." I stretch my neck to read the title, *Healthy Lives for Healthy Livestock*.

"Not now," says Caroline, without lifting her eyes.

Mom is too deep in her book to answer. She is always a mom, but now she is thinking like a

vet, so I know better than to keep trying for her attention.

"I miss Annabelle Fair already," I say to Caroline. "Don't you?" The Fairs were not only our upstairs neighbors, they were also our family's oldest friends—especially Caroline and Annabelle, who are thirty-nine days apart.

Caroline looks up from her phone. "I asked you not to say her name out loud. It makes me miss her too much."

"What if I call her *Am-hmll-hmll*?"

"Stop it."

After another minute I say, "I can't help thinking about the good times we've had with all the Fairs. Like playing Hot Potato, and how you and *Am-hmll-hmll* were both Jetpack Pandas in the Halloween play." I sigh. "It's not my fault I'm thinking about a girl whose name rhymes with Hannibal Hair."

Now Caroline looks straight-up mad. "And

now I'm thinking about a kid whose name rhymes with Waleb Wingram."

"Caleb Ingram," I say quickly, to show her I got it.

Speaking Caleb's name out loud is painful. Maybe Caroline has a point about keeping names inside. Caleb has been my best friend since preschool. Last week, in our final Doodle Jot Draw class, I laughed so hard at Caleb's doodle of two hamblings holding umbrella drinks that my chin hit my desk, and even then I couldn't stop laughing.

I'll never get to bump my elbow against Caleb's elbow at Doodle Jot Draw class again. This summer, he went to sleepover camp with no online, just postcards.

Goodbye, Caleb Ingram. Goodbye, Doodle Jot Draw class.

Goodbye, fabulous Fair family. Goodbye, neighborhood gingko trees. Goodbye, everything from my old life. I hope Nicholas isn't still teary.

As soon as we get to Blackberry Farm, I better start looking for some hellos.

CHAPTER 3

Newish Oldish

"TEXT DAD TO SEE IF OUR TRAIN IS GOING TO BEAT THE CAR!"
I say.

"We just checked a few minutes ago," says Mom.

"But our times are so close, and we're pulling
in now! Check again!"

"Becket, hush! Also, I don't have a signal."
Mom pockets her phone.

Even though Mom sounds annoyed with me,
she uses my new name so easily. Like it's never
been anything else.

The country station where we get off looks

totally different from the city one where we boarded. It's a small wooden house with a bench and a line of tracks out front. Mom and Caroline and I have just sat down on the bench to wait for Dad when an old man next to us asks Mom for the time.

"Almost three o' clock," says Mom, checking her watch.

"Stranger Danger!" I nudge Mom. "Don't talk to people you don't know."

Mom shakes her head. "It's fine. Also, lower the volume, sweetie."

Are there different rules in the country about Stranger Danger? That seems pretty risky. My palms go sweaty and my heart pounds.

When the old man's ride comes to pick him up, he shuffles off. He doesn't look too dangerous in motion—but it could be part of his act.

"Country life sure is quiet," I say.

"Not with you in it," murmurs Caroline.

"Sit tight," says Mom. "Dad's only a minute away."

"Nobody is ever a minute away."

And just like I predicted, it takes 447 seconds.

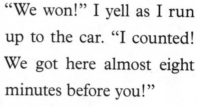

"We won!" I yell as I run up to the car. "I counted! We got here almost eight minutes before you!"

"Rebecca, you will need to lower the volume," says Dad.

"Mom already lowered my volume, and my name is Becket."

"What?" Dad trades a look with Mom.

"It's Becket's decision," says Mom.

"Okay, we can discuss it later." But Dad is looking at Mom, not me. So I know it's not all-the-way okay. I was named after Dad's great aunt Rebecca, who died before I was born. It's like my name belongs a little bit to her, too.

Or at least, I know that's how Dad sees it.

In the car, I put down my window. Afternoon sunshine feels warm and the air smells like honeysuckles. I lean my face into the breeze, close my eyes, and imagine running down that Country Goods hill with my dog—who I've decided to call Noble—at my side. My two favorite types of dogs are Labradors, because they're so friendly, and German shepherds, because they're trusted by police and blind people. My not-so-favorite type of dog is Mr. Fancypants. He's a pug and he's been around since before I was born. Mr. Fancypants only likes naps, snacks, and Nicholas—probably since Mr. Fancypants and Nicholas are both scared of lightning and need to have their food cut up into tiny pieces because they have reflux issues.

Now that we're in the country, I hope we'll get a genuine, tail-wagging country dog. I've wanted one for so long. Mr. Fancypants won't care. I doubt he'd even wake up to notice.

On the way to the farm, we stop by the Old Post Road Animal Clinic. We've been here before when Dr. Plumb was the vet. Gran was friends with Dr. Plumb and she took all her animals to him until he retired. The Old Post Road Animal Clinic is very different from my parents' city clinic, which had automatic doors and a view of the street. This clinic is at the end of a dirt road. It looks more like a house, with a covered porch, a barn, and kennels out back. Mom and Dad have been fixing it up, and now it's as cozy as a pair of socks. One whole wall in the back office is pictures of us, and our two living room armchairs and rug make the waiting room feel like home.

They proudly show us around. Then, it's back in the car.

Except for Christmases and two weeks in the summers, we Branches haven't spent much time at Blackberry Farm. A few roads are familiar and others seem brand new. But as soon as I see the flag, I know we're close.

Behind the store, Blackberry Farm spreads out

wide. There's the main farmhouse, the henhouse, the chicken run, the pony barn, and the silo where grain is kept. In the farthest field, I see Farmer Jack on his tractor. Gran and Farmer Jack share farmland for planting corn and grain. Farmer Jack also helps stock the store with his dairy's milk, cheese, and yogurt.

Gran is standing outside the farmhouse's red-painted front door, where her sunflowers are blooming. Gran reminds me of a sunflower. She is tall and cheerful and planted strong to the ground in her cork sandals.

"Beautiful Alert!" I call as I hop out of the car. I like to say that when I see something beautiful. "Gran, your sunflowers look so happy!"

Except—are they her flowers anymore? Gran is moving to the apartment above the farm store to give us space. After she hugs me, we look at her flowers. Then we go into the kitchen. "Hey, Gran," I ask, "are you sad that we're kicking you out of your home?"

"We're not—" Dad starts.

"Heck, no!" Gran cuts in. "It suits me two times over. I love my family, and I also love a change."

"Me too!"

"Can I go see my bedroom?" asks Caroline. "My own private bedroom?"

"Of course," says Gran. "This is your home now."

Mom looks up from where she's unpacking plates. "Put anything that seems like storage or trash outside your bedroom door. I'll come help you later."

Caroline races upstairs, but I stay to visit with Gran. I bet it's strange for her to have all this new furniture jammed and jigsawed into her house. Dad and Mom were hoping that Gran might declutter some of her things before we got here. Looks like that hasn't happened yet.

"Woo-wee. What a lot of stuff," Gran says, as if she's heard my thoughts. "It kind of crept up on me."

"Yeah," I say. "It's way messier than I remember!"

Gran laughs. Mom looks embarrassed and says, "Becket, upstairs."

But I know Gran likes a loud truth more than soft politeness. That's why we get along.

My new bedroom was Gran's old sewing room, but there hasn't been a sewing machine in it for a long time. "Hello, new room!" I say. "Hey, two cute windows. Hi, yellow-and-blue braided oval rug. Hello, bed just for me. Hi, bookcase."

It feels empty, though. Instead of two twin beds, I see just one, and it looks really old-fashioned. And these stacks of newspapers in the corner are not getting a happy hello from me.

"Do we need to keep these old newspapers?" I shout over the banister.

"Now why would you need a key to the zookeepers?" Gran calls up. She is slightly deaf at long distances.

"NEWSPAPERS!" I yell. "CAN I THROW THEM OUT?"

"YES!" she yells back.

My parents are wrong. I don't always need to lower the volume. Sometimes with Gran, I need to UP THE VOLUME.

Gran is a collector, just like me—but her collections are newspapers, as well as paper bags of fabric and yarn and cardboard and magazines and hangers. I'm still putting stuff in the hall when Nicholas comes charging in.

"My room's got bugs in it!"

"Oh, no! Not worse than silverfish?" In the city, sometimes we had a silverfish problem. They are not actual fish but wriggly bugs that lived in our walls.

"Double worse! These ones are dead! On my windowsill!"

I get some toilet paper and follow him. Nicholas's room is Dad's old bedroom. It's still got Dad's boyhood stuff in it, his bunk bed and his atlas wallpaper and his square Pine-O-Matic pillow stuffed with pine needles that smells so good. I forget about the bugs so I can drop down to my knees to press my nose into the Beautiful Alert pine smell.

"Stop smelling! These bugs need graves!"

I look up. "Hello, dead stinkbugs!"

Nicholas scoots behind Clive while I pinch up the dead stinkbugs with toilet paper. Then I run down the hall to drop them in the toilet. They feel dry and light and brittle, like picking up packing peanuts.

Nicholas isn't doing anything, but the whole time he looks like he might throw up.

"Thanks," says Nicholas when I'm done. "I saw a mouse outside! It almost ran over my sneaker! So gross! Remember when our school closed the kitchen because of mice?"

"Mice should not live in a school kitchen, but they *are* allowed to live outside. You can't get upset when mice are just hanging out *where they belong,* Nicholas. The outdoors is their home. Think of them all as Mrs. Frisby."

Nicholas doesn't look convinced. "I already miss the sound of sirens," he says. "And I wish the food truck would pull up. I want steamed dumplings so bad."

"What if you got yourself a country nickname? Something that makes you feel cool and different, so you don't remind yourself of a city kid?"

He shakes his head. "Nicholas is all that I am." Then he takes Clive's bow and begins to play a tune that's probably called "Sirens and Dumplings."

At the other end of the hall, I hear Caroline's voice. When I peek into her new room—Gran's used-to-be guest room—Dad's already hung her new wildflower curtains in all three of her windows. The adorable brass bear lamp from our old apartment is on her bedside table. She's opening her boxes while on a FaceTime call with Annabelle, who is helping to tell her where to put things. It's the first time all day that Caroline looks happy.

As soon as Caroline sees me, she yells "Privacy privacy privacy!" in a loud, urgent voice like I'm doing something terrible to her, and she makes big hand motions for me to leave. On the phone, I hear Annabelle laughing.

I point to the bear lamp and mouth *how come you got that?* Caroline shakes her head and kind of pushes me out the door.

Okay! Whatever! She'll miss me soon enough. Once she's off the phone with Annabelle, she'll want to come see my room and how perfectly cute I've made it. And I know I'll keep it a lot neater, too!

Back to work, I open my moving box marked PENGUINS. They traveled together because that's how penguins like to do things. I've been collecting stuffed animal penguins for years. Caroline says I'm obsessed with penguins and she's probably right, but penguins are so wonderful, I think it's weird *not* to be obsessed with penguins.

All in place, they take up half
my bed.

Next I line up my hammies
and hamblings on the dresser.
They're so glad to be out of their
suitcase they go bananas, squeaking their secret
hammy language until they understand I'm not
playing with them. Then they are quiet.

On the top of my bookcase, I arrange my
eighty-four pencil-top erasers. They're very small

and don't take up a lot of space when I get them
all lined up like soldiers. I'd never have started
collecting erasers if Caleb didn't also collect them.
We'd give them to each other as gifts when one
would ask the other to borrow a pencil. They are
shaped to look like food and cute animals, but I
haven't collected any new ones since Caleb gave
me his best, a smiling slice of purple-frosted toast

called Huckleberry Pop, right before he left for camp.

Next are my seven glasses cases. I just have one pair of eyeglasses at a time, but whenever I visit Dr. Pytlak's ophthalmologist office, I get to pick out a new case. Now I've got a collection, and I never say no to a collection. Even if this one is slightly accidental.

All done. I step back. My collections look fantastic. But my room is so quiet! In the city, Caroline and I didn't just share a room—we shared a view and knock-knock jokes and fluffy socks and ghost stories.

"Do you want to come see my room?" I ask, standing in her doorframe.

"PRIVACY!" Caroline isn't on the phone anymore. "Get out get out get out!" I guess she's not missing me yet.

"Cheese and crickets, I got it, Caroline!"

Dad is in my room when I come back. "Look, it's a waddle of penguins!" he says. He's holding boxes marked with my old name. "It's a colony of penguins! A rookery of penguins!"

"Look, it's a vanishing of Dads!" I point my finger at the door, but just as a joke. I don't have a privacy problem like Caroline, kicking me out of her room the minute she finally gets one. "Why is Caroline being such a jerk?"

"Change is hard. I think each of you kids might have different moments this summer when it really sinks in that moving is a big deal," says Dad. "Go easy on her, and on Nicholas. I'll be saying the same things to them about you."

"Except change isn't hard for me," I remind him.

"Good to know, Rebecca." Dad picks up some trash bags and leaves.

"Becket," I call after him. See? I can even change my name, easy as a snap.

After I put away my clothes and shoes and books, I tiptoe down the hall and put my ear to Caroline's closed door. Then I open it just a tiny crack. She is sitting on the floor, looking at her old yearbook. I shut the door and go back into my own room, where I sit on my bed and flip open my notebook.

"Change My Name" looks pretty good at number two on my list. Then I add "to Becket" and it looks even better.

But my list needs work. I retrace numbers one  through ten using my gold marker for more pop. At the bottom of the paper, I draw Noble and me running down a hill, just like in the Country Goods Farm Markets billboard. He looks kind of like a very small horse, or a giant squirrel. I'm not great at drawing dogs yet.

Oh, well, when I get the real Noble, I'll do a better portrait.

There's still a lot of blank space on this paper.

And that's when I get my next great idea.

CHAPTER 4

Same Faces, New Places

A GREAT IDEA NEEDS THE PERFECT TIME AND PLACE to launch it.

So when Mom calls us for dinner, I run outside. I have to set the mood. I gather purple thistles and yellow buttercups and put them in a jam jar for a table centerpiece. I fold white paper napkins into swans. I'd learned how to do this on my favorite

36

TeenyTinyCrafts channel. When I'm done, it looks like a professional restaurant.

"Beautiful Alert! At Blackberry Farm, flowers aren't just for restaurants!" I say. "Flowers are for anytime you want people to be in a good mood."

"The flowers are free, and so are the salads." Caroline lets me take a two-second peek at her bowl of lettuce, cucumbers, and tomatoes that she's picked from the garden. "At least we'll be healthy bumpkins."

"That salad needs cheese," I tell her.

"Nobody else wants cheese," says Caroline. But Mom puts some cheddar cubes in a saucer just for me. I take Punkin out of my pocket and set him on a chair I've made from a matchbox, and I put a tiny piece of cheese in his paw.

"This is *not* how we sat at home," says Nicholas, looking around. "I sat there." He points to me.

"I like my new place," I say, "because it's between Punkin and Gran."

"Your new place is my old place and that's not fair," says Nicholas.

"Pregnant ladies or people with canes are the only ones you should give up a seat for," I tell him. "You're neither. So, I'm staying put."

"Can I be excused?" Caroline asks after a couple of minutes. Her plate is clean. "I just want to go call some friends back home."

"This is home," I say.

Caroline is looking at Mom, who nods.

"My food tastes weird facing this way," says Nicholas when she's gone.

"Sit in Caroline's place," I suggest.

He slides over. "That didn't work. My stomach hurts." He looks like he might cry. Mom and Dad give me sad eyes.

"Ugh, fine! But only because you're ruining my dinner." I jump out of my seat to switch with Nicholas.

Nicholas sighs a thank you. He reaches for a roll and eats it in two bites to show how good his food tastes facing the right way.

With Caroline gone and Nicholas being a baby, the moment feels right to remind my parents which kid is doing the best job so far at country life—and to launch my great idea.

"I was thinking I could start taking care of the farm animals," I say. "Like the chickens, and Pickle and Chew."

"That's a great plan, Rebecca!" says Dad.

"Becket," I remind him.

"Because your mom and I were just talking about how to divide chores around here," says Dad.

Mom beams. "Maybe Nicholas can help. Might get him in a country spirit."

"Sure," I say. Except Nicholas looks like he wants to crawl under his plate. "Also, when you see how responsible I am . . ." I take a breath. "Then can I get a dog?"

"Becket, what?" Mom tilts her head. "I feel like we've had this conversation a few times already."

"We've only had that conversation in the city."

"I'm just surprised you'd bring it up again, since as you've noticed, we have so many more animals to take care of. And *especially* considering we already have a dog," says Mom.

I look over at Mr. Fancypants, who is lying on his back snoring like a buzz saw. I don't want to insult him, even if he is too deaf to hear, about how he's not a real country dog, or how he hasn't been a fun dog for years, since he's become too blind to fetch, too stiff to cuddle, and too grumpy to please unless you've got snacks. "Mr. Fancypants is fourteen and a half years old. Also, he belongs to Nicholas," I say carefully.

"No, he just likes me best," says Nicholas, "because I understand him."

"We have too much going on right now to get a new dog," says Dad.

It's a good thing Gran is facing my way so she can give me her secret wink. That's the wink she uses to let me know she's on my side. "If you ask me, I think it's terrific that Becket wants to show responsibility for all our animals," says Gran. "Remember, William, being a team player and helping to take care of the farm and all our animals was how you proved you were ready for Patches."

"Aw, Patches." Dad smiles. "She was a good dog."

"How old were you when you got Patches?"

"He was ten," answers Gran before Dad can speak.

"I'm ten in October," I say. "That's pretty close."

"Let's start you on chores tomorrow," says Gran briskly. "I'll show you the ropes."

I give Gran my best wink back although I can't do it crisp like her. Gran might have some clutter in her home, but there isn't any in her mind.

"All right," says Dad slowly. "First some chores . . . and then we'll see."

"*We'll see* is pretty good," I tell Punkin. "It doesn't squash the dream!"

After dinner, Caroline comes downstairs to help clean up, and then Gran heats a pot of hot chocolate while we pick a movie. Nicholas chooses his favorite, *Attack of the Zernoks*. Although we've all seen it a million times, we go along with it, even Caroline, though she texts on her phone the whole time.

"Thanks, sweetie," Mom whispers in my ear as little purple aliens swarm across the TV screen. "This is all a big adjustment for your brother. I think he needs the extra comfort. You do so much better with adventure and change."

"I know. That's what I was saying to Dad."

I look over at Nicholas. He has scooped Mr. Fancypants off his cushion, and now they are curled on the couch together. Mr. Fancypants's neck is angled just so on the crook of Nicholas's elbow, and Nicholas is drinking hot chocolate through a bendy straw, the only way he likes. They look as comfortable as two extremely picky friends can look.

Gran has also popped a bowl of popcorn, and she stays for the whole movie. She and I snuggle up on the recliner, pulling Gran's quilt over us.

When I give Gran a squeeze, she seems littler than I remember. It makes me feel protective.

Outside, the big old moon is glowing yellow over the fields.

"Beautiful Alert," I whisper.

CHAPTER 5

Animal Nature

I WAKE UP EARLY TO THE SOUND OF SQUAWKING. WHEN I look out my window, I see a poor little bird flying in clumsy loops. That's not right! It must be sick or injured! Every few seconds, the bird looks like it's going to crash.

Gran is out by the berry bush, picking blueberries and dropping them into her little red pail. Why isn't she more worried?

I'm downstairs and out of the house in a flash. "Call 911!" I yell as I start running in my own circles. "Danger, danger! Bird in trouble! We need to get that poor bird over to Mom and Dad, pronto!"

Gran looks up and shades her eyes with a hand. "It's just a little baby hawk learning to fly."

"Wait, what? Really?" I stop and watch. Now I see. The squawking must be the hawk's parents giving instructions. The baby hawk is only testing his wings.

He's going to be just fine. No crash landings.

Time to take a breath and check in on the morning. The air smells clean like cut grass. I see green apples on the apple trees and the meadow is full of blue flowers that Gran says are chicory. I shout so many Hellos and Beautiful Alerts that my voice gets hoarse.

"Ready to give Pickle and Chew their breakfast?" asks Gran as we drop off the berry-full pail in the kitchen. "Animals have to eat first, you know."

"Um, sure." Now that it's

morning, I'm nervous. Pickle and Chew are Gran's donkey and mule. As I recall, they're both cranky. And the henhouse has got its own set of problems.

But I'm a country kid now. I can handle any animal, right?

Together, Gran and I walk up the path to the pony barn. Gran pours out two buckets of breakfast oats. We add water, because Pickle and Chew both are so old that their teeth have gone soft. Gran unhooks two round brushes from the tack board.

"These are curry combs," says Gran. "After Chew and Pickle are done eating, you can groom them. Keep your eyes peeled. Check for rashes, cuts, bites, and dry patches."

"And report on any suspicious activity," I tell her. "If you see something, say something. That's always a good rule."

Gran nods. "Exactly."

I copy Gran's circle-rub style. I keep my hand steady on Pickle's backside as I walk around her. But I have to jump to avoid her kick.

"Donkeys can kick at any angle," says Gran. "Even sideways."

"I'll remember that," I say. "I am filing it under suspicious activity."

"And animal nature," adds Gran.

When we're finished, Gran gives me two carrots. "Let them know you're friends." I feed each animal from my hand. Their mouths feel so alive, it tickles my palm.

"Good job," says Gran. "Think you can do this alone from now on?"

"Sure." Then I make myself say it, even though my skin prickles. "Let's go collect the eggs."

Gran gives me a look. "Are you sure? Last visit, you ran out of the henhouse like your hair was on fire."

"I know." I close my eyes and try to replace that embarrassing memory with the picture I drew of Noble, dog of my dreams. How will I get a dog if

I'm jumpy and squeamish about other animals? "I wasn't as country, back then."

Gran keeps ninety-seven chickens in her flock, which give about eighty eggs a day. That's a lot of chickens—and as Gran says, it's hard to predict what they'll do. The reason I ran out of the henhouse last visit was because Gran's prize New Hampshire Red hen, Laying Godiva, pecked my leg so hard she left marks like pinholes. They stayed so long I got to show them to Caleb when we came back to the city.

But that was then. Now: No more being chicken about chickens!

When they see us coming, the chickens begin to cluck and squabble. A few hurry past us, ducking out of the henhouse to strut around the run. Others jump into their nesting beds. Archie, Gran's white Muscovy duck who helps to protect the henhouse, honks a friendly hello.

On her perch at the end of the coop, Laying Godiva ruffles her red feathers and gives me her meanest bull's-eye stare.

I pecked your leg, says her stare. *I might do it again.*

Even roosting, Godiva is one of the tallest hens. She is also one of Gran's best because she checks the three boxes of Gran's "r" list—robust, reliable, and ribbons. *Robust* means that Godiva can handle any weather from hot summer days to rain and snow. *Reliable* means that there's usually an egg in her nest. *Ribbons* means good-looking. Ribbons is not as important a category as the other two, but plump, tawny, feathery Godiva is a lot easier on the eye than some of Gran's more frizzle-feathered and scrawnier-necked breeds.

Too bad Godiva also checks that final "r" on my own private list: Rude!

Gran hands me a basket. "We'll wash all the eggs after we collect them."

There's lots of eggs in the nests. White, pale

green, soft blue, sand, gold, golden brown, reddish brown, and medium brown. The tinge of the egg depends on the breed of the hen. Gran's henhouse has lots of variety.

I am super-careful to take from nests that only have eggs, no hens. Gran is braver. She can slip her hand under the broody hens to get their eggs.

At one empty nest, I reach in carefully for two reddish-brown eggs and—

"YOUCH!" Laying Godiva! She races up and pecks me so quick I don't have time to dodge. "MY THUMB!"

The mark on my thumb is bright red. "She fooled me again!"

Gran scoops up her hen. "There, now." She makes that special *tsk tsk* noise she uses for comforting her chickens.

"*I'm* the one who got pecked! Why is Laying Godiva so mean to me?"

"Godiva just gets rattled," says Gran. "Chickens have lots of emotions."

"Godiva's main emotion is rage."

"Fear, more likely. She's a chicken, and it's her animal nature to size you up," says Gran. "Meantime, giving your chicken a cuddle can do her a world of good."

There's no way Godiva would ever let me hold her like Gran does, hand under her bum and close against Gran's side. If that's a cuddle, count me out.

Godiva's got her eye on me, but I'm not playing her game. I drop our staring contest first.

Gran and I leave the henhouse with eighty-eight eggs in all. We rinse, dry, and box them into seven egg cartons to sell at Branch's.

"With four eggs left over to make egg salad sandwiches," says Gran.

"Or a butter cake." I love Gran's butter cake, because it's not too sweet.

"How are you feeling about your first day of chores?" she asks.

I think about that. I can probably handle a kicking donkey and a noisy henhouse. I'm not so sure about Laying Godiva. But a real country kid doesn't run away from a big fat hen. A country kid stays calm.

At my old school, Mrs. Wallerby, our crossing guard, made a hand signal with one arm raised up and her fingers motioning the okay whenever it was time to cross the street. Everyone followed Mrs. Wallerby's signals, because she always looked kind, sensible, and correct.

I do one of Mrs. Wallerby's hand signals now. "Easy peasy mac and cheesy," I say. "These chores have officially crossed over to being my responsibility."

Gran gives me her wink. "Attagirl."

CHAPTER 6

No Pink, No Polka Dots

EVERYBODY'S IN THE KITCHEN WHEN I COME INSIDE. DAD IS making his from-scratch pancakes using Gran's fresh-picked blueberries.

"Three pancakes for me, please!" My thumb already feels better.

Dad makes his pancakes with buttermilk. It's a secret ingredient that everyone knows about.

Still, Dad's "mystery" pancakes are a Branch family treat that we only get once in a while. Dad makes them either when we've done something good or when something bad is about to happen.

I close my eyes to savor their fluffy warm blueberry pancake goodness and hope the only thing behind this breakfast is a cozy farm welcome. But my stomach also gets that ant-crawling feeling that bad news is ahead.

Mom saves it until we're stuffed full and licking the sticky bits of syrup off our fingers.

"Becket and Nicholas, listen up," she says, folding her hands in an arch. Her face looks serious too.

"Uh-oh." Nicholas is the twin who dreads things. I'm the twin who gets excited for them. I'm sort of surprised that he didn't sense it was coming.

"What is it?" I ask.

"Dad and I have signed you both up for Young Explorers summer day camp. They've just sent me a list of the supplies you'll need. Since today's a light day at the clinic, I thought I'd take off the morning so we can go into town and shop."

"*Camp?*" But this whole farm feels more like a camp than Camp Easy Breeze, where Nicholas and I went last year.

"I don't like camp!" shouts Nicholas. His eyes are already red. It's never too early in the day for Nicholas to cry.

"I loved Young Explorers when I was a kid," says Dad. "It's got a creek you can swim in. The hiking trails are really cool. You'll get to meet a bunch of kids. Also, while Mom and I are at work, we'll be happy knowing you aren't just sitting around."

"Last summer in the city, you won Camp Easy Breeze's Spirit Award, remember, Becket?" says Mom.

"Yup." I nod. Camp Easy Breeze was fun, but

I keep my face a secret. I want to see how bad Nicholas reacts first. Nicholas is a "squeaky wheel," which means that if he gets really unhappy, then my parents will try to give him special extras to put him in the right mood. Squeaky-wheeling has been working a lot for Nicholas lately. Like getting to sit where he wants at the table or picking his favorite movie. So maybe this is a good opportunity for me to be not so much of a smooth wheel.

"Are you both nuts? I'm not good at camp *at all*," reminds Nicholas. "This will be pure torture!"

"Young Explorers is only half days," says Mom. "Dad will drop you both off in the morning, and I'll pick you up later in the afternoon. Afternoons, you're free as a lark."

Caroline is keeping her eyes on her fork as she skates her last bite of pancake through maple syrup.

"Is Caroline doing camp, too?" I ask.

"Caroline is almost twelve—old enough to help out at the store," says Dad. "So she'll be working there in the mornings with Gran."

"Look, I'm fine to go to camp, but just to remind

you, this was not on my list, folks!" I say. "You didn't tell Nicholas and me one thing about throwing us away into Young Explorers Camp. I feel like you owe us *both* a big one, if we have to go there."

"We're not throwing you anywhere. We're placing you gently. Young Explorers is down the road, over at Boggs Hollow Elementary, where I went to school and where you'll be going this fall," says Dad.

"I'm young. I explore. I'm *already* a Young Explorer," I remind him. "I'm agreeing to go to this camp because I am also a team player."

Nicholas is so upset he runs upstairs. We all hear the slam of his door and then he does some thudding around.

"Heeeere we go," says Mom. Sure enough, soon the weepy scrape of "Thrown Away into Camp" cello music floats down to us.

"Thanks for being a good sport, Becket," says Mom. "Knowing you, by next week you'll be on your way to your next Spirit Award."

But Mom can't smooth-wheel me away that

easy. "Maybe, but maybe not. The important thing to remember here is how mature I'm being, even though I don't want to go to camp, either." And since I don't have a Clive, I scrape my chair hard from the table and clear my plate using as much noise as it takes, plus a little extra. Smooth wheels can squeak a little, too!

Mom goes upstairs. After a few minutes, she comes down with a smile and with Nicholas, who is dressed for the day.

"Nicholas and I are going into town to get brand-new cool camping supplies."

Nicholas looks guilty. Shopping is his weakness. That's how Mom tempted him. "Get dressed quick and come along?"

"No, thanks. Just get double of whatever supplies Nicholas gets."

"No outer space stuff or orange, right?" asks Nicholas.

"Pick out anything, I don't care." Shopping is not my weakness.

But after they drive away, I think about how

bleh I'd feel if they came back with outer space or orange. I go find Caroline.

"Get out of my room, please," she says.

"Cheese and crickets, I'm just in the doorway. Can you text Mom no outer space and no orange, no pink including hot pink, no mermaids, no princesses or fairies, no reptiles, no polka dots, no stripes?"

"Got it, now go away, go go go." Caroline is like an evil queen in the kingdom of her new room. I know it was the main thing she was looking forward to about moving, but why does she have to rub it in so hard?

Like it was such a torture to share a room with me!

"Okay, but also just text yes to all greens except mint green, yes to rainbows, yes to baby hamsters, baby turtles, baby penguins, yes to puppies especially German shepherd puppies, yes to erasers with faces—"

"This text is way, way too long," says Caroline. "You should have gone with Mom and Nicholas if you want stuff just right. I don't have to do this. I'm not your babysitter." But she comes out into the hall—no way will she invite me into her precious room—and we sit at the top of the steps, texting with Mom until she's found everything I need.

"I gotta go down to the store," says Caroline, clicking her phone off.

"Can I go?"

I take her shrug to mean yes. In my room, I change into my rainbow shirt and jeans shorts. I stick Punkin into the hatband of a cute straw hat I find in my closet. I make sure his eyes are peeking out so he knows what's going on.

Halfway to the store, I have to take my glasses off and rub the lenses in case my eyes are playing tricks.

He is tied by a leash to a tree outside. He is even more perfect than I imagined. Pale gold with white markings on his face and paws. Warm, smart, chocolate eyes. Soft, floppy ears and a long, brushy tail.

Noble, my country dog, has leapt out of my billboard and is standing right in front of me.

CHAPTER 7

¡Hola, Oro!

THERE'S A SIGN OUTSIDE BRANCH'S DOOR THAT READS PUSH HARD.

I do—maybe too hard. The door slams against the wall as the antique doorbell tings overhead to let Gran know when a customer is here. But I need to know who belongs to that dog right away!

Inside, it's dark and cool just like I remember. I take a deep breath of that familiar scent of fresh-baked bread and brown sugar. Some of the best Beautiful Alerts happen through the nose.

Gran signals me to the front counter. "I'm

giving Caroline a cash register lesson," she says. "Want to learn?"

"She might be too young," says Caroline.

"Punkin will help," I say. "He's great at math." I scoot next to them behind the register, but my eyes are watching the dog owners. They're the only customers in the store—a man and woman by the freezer section, along with a girl who might be my age. Her skin is a couple of shades darker than my peach tone skin, and her hair is a coppery-brown puff held back in a headband. She's wearing a dress with sparkles on it. A sparkly dress wouldn't be something I'd pick for myself, but I know a Beautiful Alert when I see one.

Is that your dog? I want to ask her. Even though I know it is.

All that happens is my face gets hot. At my old school, I'd known everyone since kindergarten. During the summer, half my school went to Camp Easy Breeze. Come to think of it, I haven't met someone new for a long time. I'm probably out of practice.

Gran is explaining about the cash register, but Punkin and I aren't paying any attention. When the girl's parents come over to set down a few things, I see that the dad has the girl's same hair, and the mom has her same tea-brown eyes.

"Good morning, Maria and Lucas! Morning, Frieda! Girls, I'd like you to meet our neighbors, the Francas, and their daughter, Frieda."

"You two girls must be about the same age," Frieda's mom says, pointing to her daughter and me.

"Becket and her twin brother, Nicholas, are both going into fourth grade at Boggs Hollow Elementary this fall," volunteers Gran.

"Just like you, Frieda!" says her dad.

Gran keeps a jar of barley-sugar lollipops by the register to hand out, and now she gives one to Frieda.

"Thanks," says Frieda.

What breed is your dog? How old is he? When did you get him? My questions are right on the tip of my tongue.

But where did my voice go?

Frieda Franca stares at me. Slowly, she unwraps her lollipop and then pokes it in her mouth. Does she want to say something to me as much as I want to say something to her?

Meantime, the Francas gather more grocery items: one carton of eggs, a bottle of milk, a bottle of half-and-half, and a tub of yogurt. The whole time, they're chatting with Gran and Caroline about the deliciousness of yogurt and other foods you can add to yogurt, like dates and granola.

Yogurt is gross, and granola cannot change that. Dates are gross, too. This is a gross conversation. I move my ears away from the register to the jams and syrups section.

Frieda Franca takes a few steps until she is right near me.

What's his name? Does he sleep outside or inside? Is he friendly? Is he smart?

I sidle over to the dry goods shelves. I try to feel how my questions would sound if they came out of my mouth instead of swirling around in my head. Frieda creeps over, too. I move to the bread shelf. Frieda again.

Can he do tricks? Did you teach him? Does he know his own name?

Frieda is standing in front of me. The words

are inside me. If I keep them in one more second, I'll explode.

"Your dog?"

Does my voice sound this shy? Did I really only say two words? Did it make a real sentence?

A smile breaks across Frieda Franca's face like it had been hiding there all along. "Yes! He's ours! He's a golden retriever puppy and his name is Oro. He's only seven months old, and he's really friendly. He sleeps in the hallway outside my bedroom, and I'm trying to teach him how to shake hands. Come say hi to him!"

It's like Frieda Franca heard every single question in my head.

Together, we bang out of the store. We run right over to where

Oro's lying down at his post. As soon as Frieda says "¡Hola, Oro!" he jumps up. He licks Frieda's chin and then mine.

He has the sweetest doggy face I ever saw. And now that we've broken the ice, Frieda and I have plenty of things to say to each other. That's how I find out that she's going to Young Explorers Camp.

"I just know we are going to be best camp friends," I tell her.

"I've never been to camp before," says Frieda.

"When I was at Camp Easy Breeze, I won for most camp spirit. So I am kind of an expert. Stick with me, I'm *great* at camp! I even get awards for it!"

"Oh, okay," says Frieda, though her smile isn't as big as I'd hoped. "Cool."

"The Francas are nice," says Caroline, after they leave.

"They're better than nice!" I shout. "That whole family is one giant Beautiful Alert!"

Gran smiles. "They are, aren't they? They're from—"

"Peru! They lived on six hundred acres of land,

but they moved here a few months ago to start an alpaca farm!"

Gran nods. "And it's—"

"Only a couple of miles away! And I can visit! Also, Frieda's going to come over to Blackberry Farm one day, so I can show her my hammies and penguins and eraser faces." I don't say anything about Frieda's other suggestion—to have Oro and Mr. Fancypants meet up for a play date. "Mr. Fancypants" and "play date" don't go together. The only playing Mr. Fancypants does is with his dog food, nosing out the liver chunks that he doesn't like.

I've just got to keep working to earn Noble. An Oro-Noble play date would be the best.

Gran laughs. "Sounds like you two will get along just fine."

"I'd love to see their farm," says Caroline. It's one of the first times I've heard her sound interested in something around here. "Alpacas are just like llamas, but half the size and with cuter ears."

I hadn't put "Find a New Best Friend" on my

list—and now here she is, Frieda Franca, with her own alpacas and bouncy dog. I wish Mr. Fancypants had a little more bounce for a play date with "Beautiful Alert" Oro. Then again, Frieda's been a country kid for longer than me. Of course she'd already have the perfect dog. It doesn't make sense to be jealous.

Except maybe I am, a little.

CHAPTER 8

Safety Tips

MOM BROUGHT HOME SOME FUN CAMP SUPPLIES FOR ME: A penguin thermos, a rainbow backpack, and a moss-green towel. Green is my favorite color since it's the color of nature (except not mint green, which reminds me of the dentist).

There's just one problem: my lunchbox. The picture of the puppy on the front looks like a sad puppy-clown-seal.

"Then you should've come shopping with us," says Mom when I start to complain. "Anyway, it was on sale." Translation: she isn't taking it back.

Nicholas has an outer space lunchbox with a silver-foil Milky Way. Even though I don't like outer space stuff, it's actually pretty cool.

But I don't care. He might have found a better lunchbox, but I already found my new best friend, Frieda Franca.

On the first morning of Young Explorers, I set my alarm so that I'm up even earlier to feed and brush Pickle and Chew. This time, it's Chew that kicks me, right on my shin—and I'm not quick enough to dodge.

Ouch! That'll be a bruise.

Next, Gran and I collect eggs from the henhouse. I refuse to make eye contact with Laying Godiva, and I don't collect any eggs near where she's roosting. But I know she's got her eye on me. I'm her Stranger Danger and she is mine.

Once I'm done, I leave that henhouse fast.

Since I'm the first awake, I also let out Mr. Fancypants. As always, he spends a few minutes blinking at the sun. Mr. Fancypants is used to hitting the pavement, and I wonder if he likes being retired from his morning walk. Then he starts coughing, which my parents say is because of his heart and his trachea, but Nicholas says it's also anxiety. So I go outside to rub his head until his coughing fit passes. Then I stay with him while he does his business. The Great Outdoors seems to confuse him.

"You'll learn to like it," I tell Mr. Fancypants. "You need to give it some time." Next, I make my delicious breakfast—toasted cheddar on bread with a smear of clover honey from Gran's friends at Bee Sweet Farm. When Mr. Fancypants comes waddling back inside, he goes bananas slurping up a tiny bit of the honey that dribbled off my spoon onto the kitchen floor. Usually we just hide Mr. Fancypants's morning heart pill in his dog bowl with breakfast—but when I take a pill and coat it in honey, he gulps it down.

Then he looks up at me for more.

"Mr. F, you're sure easy to trick," I tell him. "But I think your taste for Bee Sweet honey puts you one paw closer to country dog status."

He sighs in agreement, eats his breakfast, and settles in for his morning nap.

When Mom comes downstairs, I help make camp lunches. I push my creepy lunchbox deep inside my backpack. This puppy-clown-seal needs to stay hidden from campers' eyes!

On the drive over to Boggs Hollow Elementary, Nicholas keeps asking Dad to change the radio stations. But he doesn't like any of the music, no matter what Dad switches to. He's just being crabby, which means he's got a case of nerves.

Sure enough, as soon as Dad checks us in and says goodbye, Nicholas wants me to find the nurse's office.

"My insides feel wobbly. I have the flu maybe," he says. "I might have a stomach virus or Mona."

"Mono," I correct. "Nicholas, all you've got in your stomach is butterflies."

Nicholas stares across the lawn of kids. "Doesn't it feel like everybody here knows everybody else?"

"That's how the beginning of anything feels," I remind him.

"¡Hola, Becket!" Frieda Franca runs up. She's wearing a sparkly peacock skirt and booties.

"Whoa, you look more like an acrobat than a camper!" I tell her. "Didn't you read what the printout said about sensible footwear? Believe me, you will regret that choice!"

Frieda frowns as she looks down at her booties. "They feel okay."

"I think you look amazing," says Nicholas.

"Thank you!" Frieda smiles at him. "I'm Frieda."

"I'm Nicholas." They start talking about clothes and shopping and how they aren't really that into camp. I just stand there, waiting for Nicholas

to look at me so I can give him eye daggers for trying to nudge in on my very first country friend. But he never looks.

Soon the counselors call us by name to divide into sections. Nicholas and I are in different sections, but he and Frieda are together.

Oh, nooo. That's not gonna work.

I march over to Counselor Paloma, who's in

charge of 3B. "Why am I in 3B and Nicholas is in 3A? We are twins. Twins don't like being separated. So I'll just scoot into 3A, if that's okay by you."

"Good morning to you, too, Rebecca Branch. I see here you are otherwise known as Becket! Actually, no section scooting, please. We do know that you and Nicholas are twins. We think you'll make new friends easier if you aren't in the same section," explains Paloma. "Luckily, you'll both be outside at noon for lunch. And you'll have neighbor time when we test our homemade boats on the stream."

"Outside lunch? And we're doing a craft? I love outside lunch and crafts!"

"A little lower, Becket," says Paloma, pretending to adjust a dial. Then she presses my nose freckle.

Pretty much anyone who meets my freckle likes to press it.

I try to catch Nicholas's eye, but he's *still* talking to Frieda. I want to feel happy that he has a friend in his section, but this is total friend-theft. Just wait till Frieda learns that Nicholas has about as much camp spirit as a toadstool.

When the bell rings for everyone to go inside, I run up the school steps and plant myself in front of the entrance. I remember all the crossing signals I learned from Mrs. Wallerby, so that everyone can proceed into the school in an orderly fashion.

"Orderly fashion!" I call. But campers just push on past me. Where are the rules here? This camp feels like chaos!

"Okay, Explorers! It's morning meeting time," says Counselor Pete once we're inside and assembled in our classroom.

Pete and Paloma start the meeting with one of my favorite topics, Safety. I'm relieved to learn that country camp has even more safety tips than city camp. We get tips on everything: sunburn, poison ivy, poison sumac, dehydration, deer ticks, mosquitoes, matches, slippery rocks, rushing water, still water, sharp rocks, why we wear life jackets, and why we wear helmets. We didn't have to worry about deer ticks or life jackets in the city.

"Do any of you want to add a tip that I might have missed?" asks Pete.

"You didn't mention Stranger Danger!" I say.

"Thanks, Becket. Luckily, nobody is a stranger here at Young Explorers Camp," says Pete.

"Don't be so sure." I shake my finger. "What if there's a wolf-man living in the forest? What if nobody has seen him since he was raised by the

friendly yet deadly wolves that cared for him after his parents died? Wolf-men are real—I saw one on the subway!"

"Okay!" Pete puts up his hands. "Stranger Danger is worth a mention."

"And just one more thing," I say. "Be careful during crafts. Especially if you are using hot glue guns. You could glue your fingers together or burn the hair off your arm skin." A camper whose name tag reads CADIE makes a sort of whimpering noise. So I finish up quick. "Stay alert, and you won't get hurt!"

I really love safety tips. They are always so inspiring.

"That was kind of scary," says Cadie, and nobody disagrees.

"Oookay, Becket. Thank you! You sure know your safety!" Paloma claps her hands. "Let's move on to some pointers about Respecting Your Neighbor."

When it's time for indoor games, it's Cadie, not me, who gets chosen to be door helper. Even though

I'm the one who understands the most about safety. Cadie doesn't know Mrs. Wallerby's hand signals, and everyone starts pushing and shoving. I'm not picked to be indoor games captain, either. That is weird, since at Camp Easy Breeze I got picked for stuff a lot. At kitchen activity, when 3A and 3B combine, I learn that Frieda and Nicholas are already paired up. I have to be Cadie's partner, and she's not very talkative. Not to me, anyway.

The whole entire morning, there hasn't been one Beautiful Alert.

"I don't know how you're feeling about camp, but I sure hope things start to improve around here," I whisper to Punkin. He stays quiet, but at least I know he's there.

CHAPTER 9

FF Freakout

"OKAY, EXPLORERS! GET READY FOR SOME CRAFTING FUN. Our next activity is making miniature boats," says Paloma.

I perk up. I am very good at tiny things. I've watched hours of TeenyTinyCrafts channel, so I know what I'm doing. We head to the cafeteria, where kids from other sections join up with us. I wave to Nicholas, but he's with Frieda plus another kid who looks big and tough.

First Nicholas steals Frieda, then he decides to be friends with the toughest-looking kid at Young

Explorers? Have alien Zernoks secretly attacked Nicholas and taken over his identity?

Spread out on the lunch tables are the materials for boat building: aluminum pans, foam board, foil, egg cartons, CDs, Popsicle sticks, and milk and orange juice containers, plus all kinds of paints and markers and stickers for decorating. They've even put out google eyes. I stick a tiny google eye on each of my eyelids and some kids laugh, but Cadie screams, and Pete tells me to take them off. "Not the right kind of attention, Becket," he says in a friendly voice.

"Okay, sorry!" I call out to show no hard feelings.

Maybe if I build the perfect boat just right for Punkin, then I'll get the right kind of attention. I study the table a long time, finding my inspiration.

Then my great idea comes, POW! I rubber-band three corks for the boat bottom, and I use two toothpicks to rig the sails, which I've cut from shiny pea-green paper.

When I'm done with building, I paint "SS *Punkinlunkin*" on the side.

Hello, Boat!

Thankfully lunch is right after. Making such a darling, perfect craft wipes me out. I keep my sad-puppy-clown-seal lunchbox hidden deep in my backpack while I pull out my sandwich, grapes, and granola bar all individually. Like they were just hanging around loose in there.

Nicholas's group is lounged out under a tree. I try to catch my brother's eye again—but nope. He's busy talking with kids. I feel so upside-down I'm dizzy. How did Nicholas get to be the center of everything? I haven't made one single friend in 3B.

The counselors have brought out some paper so that after lunch, we can stay outside to talk to people or do leaf rubbings, or both. I'd rather talk to new friends, but since none have shown up, I'm glad that leaf rubbings are a total Beautiful Alert of art and nature. I love 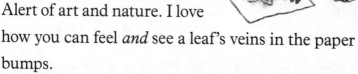 how you can feel *and* see a leaf's veins in the paper bumps.

When everyone has finished cleaning up after lunch hour, we drop off our art at sections 3A and 3B. Then we watch a short video called *Love Those Bugs*, about how insects help the ecosystem. Nicholas keeps his hands over his eyes the whole time, but nobody tells him he is acting like a baby.

It's like everyone at Young Explorers totally gets my brother, even though they don't really know him yet.

After the video, we collect our boats before heading back outside. I join Nicholas and his new friends to walk down to the stream.

"Oh, hey, Becket. Are you going to hang out with us?" asks Nicholas.

"Only because I want to see how you're doing," I answer. "I'd be totally fine to hang out in my own section, too, because it's fantastic."

"Meet Zane," says Nicholas, as Zane grunts. "He's my new friend. And you already know Frieda."

"Yeah, sure! How's Oro, Frieda? How are your alpacas? Did you get any postcards from Peru, where your grandparents live?" I want to show Nicholas that I know plenty of things about Frieda.

Frieda shrugs. "They usually just write me emails."

Zane is two heads taller than Nicholas. He is a size XXL kid from head to toe. "Who wants to bet a dollar my boat will win?" he asks me.

Finally, a chance to win the day! "Me me me," I say. "My boat's built for speed."

"I'm not the betting type," says Nicholas.

"I'm not, either," says Frieda.

"I am," says Zane.

"I am times two," I tell him. "Back where I'm from, kids called me Bet-it Branch."

Nicholas rolls his eyes but he doesn't tell everybody I just made that up.

At the lake, we put our boats on the water. Frieda has created an incredibly beautiful boat. It's an all-bark raft with three leaf sails that she decorated with silver glitter dots. How did she do that? It's so delicate and pretty. She launches it with a gentle drop into the current.

"Go FF *Freedom!*" she calls.

"You mean SS *Freedom*," says Zane. "*SS* stands for steamship."

"I like FF better!" Frieda smiles. "It's my initials."

"I got that as soon as you said it," I tell her. "FF is way smarter than SS." Frieda smiles even wider.

She is so friendly with everyone. It makes me itchy trying to figure out what I can do to be special for Frieda Franca.

Zane made a sponge boat called the SS $, and Nicholas made a half-tennis-ball boat that he didn't even bother to name. It's like Nicholas already knows his boat will get caught on rocks and be the first one out of the race.

"SS *Punkinlunkin* picked up a breeze!" I yell. I follow my boat and poke it with a long stick whenever it spins around. "Forecast predicts a win for *Punkinlunkin!*"

We all run shouting after our boats as they wobble and spin down the stream. Then Frieda's boat catches a downriver current and starts heading for the rapids.

"Don't worry!" I tell her. "I'll help!" But when I give her boat a nice strong push, it capsizes and one of the leaf sails falls off in a sad spin of green and glitter.

"Ohhh, noooo!" yells Cadie. "Becket just destroyed Frieda's boat!"

Other kids are saying "nooo!" and "uh-ohhh!" and one kid mutters, "Klutz."

"Oh my gosh, Frieda, I'm so sorry!" My cheeks are bright and hot. How did I let that happen?

"Don't worry about it," says Frieda in her same sweet voice.

Now it's down to the SS *$* and the SS *Punkinlunkin*, but it's hard for me to stay excited. When a sudden puff of breeze almost flips Zane's boat, I'm sure victory is mine—but then his boat rights itself and whirls ahead, gliding far ahead of the SS *Punkinlunkin* for the win.

"Holla for a dolla!" yells Zane, shoving out his hand.

"I don't have any money on me," I admit. It doesn't seem like the time to tell Zane I don't have any money, period.

"Then you. Owe. Me." Zane pushes his face up so close he fogs my glasses. I smell granola bar on his breath.

"Sorry about your boat, Frieda," says Nicholas as we all head back.

"It's okay," says Frieda quietly. "I can always make another one."

"I'm double sorry," I say. "I feel really bad. I'm going to make it up to you, promise!"

"Okay, cool," says Frieda in that same easygoing way. I don't want to give up on my imagination billboard, with its picture of me and Frieda in the sunshine, running alongside our dogs, Oro and Noble. But real life feels so different.

At pickup, Mom and Gran are together in the car.

"How was your first day at Young Explorers?" asks Mom as we pull out.

"I knew the most safety tips. I learned a lot about bugs. And I made a boat, the SS *Punkinlunkin*. Also, here!" I give my leaf rubbing to Gran.

"Thank you! What a thoughtful piece of art," says Gran.

"Nice job, Becket," says Mom.

"I MADE TWO FRIENDS!" Nicholas never talks loud. He wants to be sure Gran hears every word. "FRIEDA AND ZANE."

"Oh, Nicholas!" says Gran. "That is wonderful!"

"You're so friendly, Nicholas, I'm not surprised," says Mom. But I can tell that she is, a little.

"It was really easy," says Nicholas. "Everyone always says 'be yourself' but this time, I really was one hundred percent Nicholas Branch, and it worked! When I talked about my allergies, my new friend Zane said he was allergic to dust, pollen, strawberries, and ragweed. That's as many allergies as me. I can eat strawberries, but not walnuts. Zane can eat walnuts, but not strawberries. Pretty cool, right?"

"You can keep Zane," I tell him. "I think Frieda and I will end up having more in common."

"Sure, as long as you don't keep wrecking her

stuff," says Nicholas as he settles back in his seat and smiles to himself.

We are both quiet for the rest of the ride.

Back home, I look at my list.

1. Goodbye, City!
2. Change My Name **to Becket**
3. Do Barnyard Chores (to Get a Country Dog)
4. Make a New Best Friend

I'd checked off everything—but now I have to change my number four. Frieda Franca is a friend, yes. But so far, not a best.

And I need to add a fifth, less-fun item to the list. I write it in bold letters.

5. **Get Rich Quick**

CHAPTER 10

Lemon Ache

"TODAY IS THE DAY!" I TELL MY FAMILY SATURDAY MORNING once I come back from the henhouse. "I just need to invent a secret lemonade recipe, so nobody better spy on me."

"Cross my heart, I won't spy." Caroline doesn't look up from the newspaper.

"Zane is coming over for our play date today," says Nicholas. "We're planning to build forts and be robot zombies. So, that's already two things better than watching you stir lemonade."

"Fine," I tell him. "But just to let you know, if

you two don't annoy me too much, then you can be my taste testers." I wish Frieda and Oro were coming over, too, but I'd already gotten Mom to call over to her house. Frieda said she was busy helping out her family today.

"She doesn't want to be my friend because I broke her boat," I say to Mom quietly when I get off the phone.

"You didn't do it on purpose," says Mom.

"She doesn't like me."

"Hey, don't let yourself get down about that," she says. "Today is still a perfect day for lemonade. But just to remind you, you'll need lemons. And check to be sure you have all the other ingredients."

"Yeah, we have everything," I say.

"Come with me to the supermarket, and I'll buy you all the lemons you want," says Dad. "Then you can give me a hand with the groceries, okay?"

Uh-oh. That sounds like a lot of work for

lemons, but since lemon trees don't grow on Blackberry Farm, I'm stuck. "Okay," I say.

Sure enough, once Dad and I hit the road, he's got a million Dad-ish morning errands he didn't tell me about. Like stopping by the bank and the gas station and the hardware store.

"You're turning my morning into boring," I tell him.

"There's a saying, 'when life gives you lemons, make lemonade,'" says Dad. "That means trying to make the best of a bad situation."

I frown. "Okay, but what if my bad situation is how hard it is to get lemons?"

"Then I guess this saying is extra perfect for you." Dad wriggles his eyebrows.

The supermarket is far away. I unroll my window and go "*Ahhhhhhhhhh*" to listen to my voice bump in the wind.

"Maybe enough of that," says Dad.

"I'm making lemonade out of this long lemony drive," I explain. "A subway could have gotten us here way faster."

"Then you'd miss out on the sunshine," says Dad.

Good point, Dad.

When we finally get home with a trunk full of groceries, I help Dad put them away, except for the high cupboards where I can't reach. Finally, the kitchen counter is clear and I can get to work. I empty the bag of lemons onto a cutting board, stopping a few before they roll onto the floor and disrupt Mr. Fancypants's nap. Then it's time to juice. I squeeze the lemons through a sieve until my hands hurt and my palms and fingers taste sour. Next, I add my secret ingredients—ripe berries from our berry patch, plus some mint! Ta-dah!

Plonk, plonk, plonk.

Raspberries, blueberries, blackberries and mint leaves all drop into the pitcher. Next go ice cubes, water, and a dollop of Bee Sweet honey. We are almost out, but I manage to scrape one last bottom-of-the-jar spoonful for Mr. Fancypants.

Berry mint lemonade, invented! This is such a great idea! I'm almost rich! I get paper napkins and paper cups from the pantry, plus a shoebox to hold my profits. Gran points out some wooden crates by the barn for me to stack into a table, and I use the leftover crate as a chair.

Gran also finds me a red-checked tablecloth so my table looks super cute.

In my tidiest letters, I make a poster board:

NOT-TOO-SWEET
3 BERRY MINT
LEMONADE
$1

And I tape the sign at the corners so it doesn't blow away.

Lastly, I bring out Mr. Fancypants on his cushion. He's not my first choice for company. In fact, he's more like my last choice, but what are my other options? I can't think too hard about

NOT-TOO-SWEET
3 BERRY MINT
LEMONADE
$1

the fact that Frieda was busy, and that Nicholas landed a play date before I did, or I'll just feel low. Mr. Fancypants wheezes and snorgles and coughs, but then he gazes up at me like he's glad for the change. Sunshine probably feels good on dogs' faces, too. He gives a big satisfied sniff, one last rearrangement of himself, then falls asleep. Soon his snores are louder than Dad's.

"You sure aren't fun, Mr. F," I tell him, "but you'd get a gold medal for naps."

When I look up, Nicholas and Zane are standing right in front of me.

"You said we could be taste testers," says Nicholas. Zane grunts.

I pour an itsy-bitsy taste into a single cup for them to share. No point in wasting my precious lemonade on non-payers.

"*PHHHFFFT*!" Zane spits out his taste. "There's no sugar in your lemonade!"

"What are you talking about?" I frown. "It's lightly sweetened with honey."

"*PHHHFFFT*!" My brother spits his sip, too. "Maybe you mean it's *barely* sweetened with honey!"

I give Nicholas the frown that I can't give to Zane, because Zane is our guest. "It's got a lemon kick!"

Nicholas takes one last sip, throws down the cup, and makes a scrunched-up face like he's a clown acting in a circus skit. "Your lemonade almost kicked my tongue out of my mouth!" It makes me so mad I could smack him.

"Yeah, you'd need first aid after this lemonade!" says Zane. Then the boys run off howling with laughter before I can think of a single excellent comeback.

I pour myself a small cup of lemonade.

Pow. Whoa. Okay, the boys were right. It's sour. But. Sour can be delicious. Sour means not too icky sweet. I take another sip, but that tastes even worse because I know exactly what kind of sour it will be. My face is all pre-scrunched for it.

The Bee Sweet jar is empty. When I check in the kitchen,

we're out of sugar, too. I should have checked my ingredients when Mom told me to. "Dad!" I call. "We forgot to pick up sugar from the grocery store!" That's when I remember Dad and Mom had gone into work for a couple of hours. Gran is the grown-up in charge.

"What do you need, sweets?" she asks when I come into Branch's Farm Store. "We were just about to have some lunch."

Caroline's expression is not as helpful.

"Can I have a sack of sugar for my lemonade stan—?"

"You know better than that!" interrupts Caroline. "Taking from the store messes up the inventory. Why can't you use honey?"

Gran nods. "Honey would be tasty."

"Okay, can I have some honey, then?" I ask. "We're out of that, too."

Caroline frowns. "No, for the same reason."

But then Gran finds me two mini honey sample jars that Bee Sweet gives out for free tastes. She also gives me a raspberry lollipop to make me feel better. "Join us upstairs, if you like. We've made a twice-baked mac and cheese, and it's heating up right now."

"Maybe." It's hard to feel overly invited when Caroline's face looks like she drank the rest of my lemonade.

Outside, I pour in the honey samples. Blerk. My pitcher's still got pucker.

My Get Rich Quick plan is taking longer than I thought, but as I unwrap my lollipop to chase away the sours, I've got another idea.

CHAPTER 11

Try, Try Again

I WAIT A FEW MINUTES BEFORE I TUCK MY SHOEBOX UNDER my arm and head back into the store. Gran and Caroline are upstairs. I hear the clanking of plates and can smell the warm waft of baking, bubbling cheese. Resisting mac and cheese turns out to be the hardest part of this plan so far.

I won't even let myself think about it. I just shake all the lollipops from Gran's glass jar by the register into my shoebox. Lollipops are free for anyone who comes into the store. So it's not like I'm stealing. Gran would never see it that way. But I'm glad Caroline is upstairs. If Caroline saw my shoebox of lollipops, she might have a different opinion. She'd definitely have a different opinion about the individual butter pound cake I pocket, but I helped Gran make these pound cakes, and a girl's gotta eat.

I can feel that tiny pinch of Bad Idea, but it's so small. Like a bug bite. I ignore it.

Outside, I set the lid on my shoebox and wait for the first car to pull in. "Get a cup of three-berry lemon-ade when you're done shop-ping," I singsong to the mom and her three little kids heading into Branch's.

"We've already had some o-range juice at break-fast," sings the mom back to me.

When they come out of the store, I've got another chance.

"Free LOLLIPOP with every kid's cup of le-mon-ade," I sing. "The kids can use the lollipop as a stirrer to add sweet-ness."

The kids start jumping around. "Please, Mom? PLEASE?"

The mom gives me a look, but then she buys four cups of lemonade.

I give one lollipop to each kid, and get four dollars in return. I fold the bills into my hatband. The kids unwrap their lollipops before they've even had a sip of lemonade, but then they seem happy for both.

When the mom takes a sip, her mouth twists. "You didn't go nuts with the sweetener, hmm?"

"Nope. That's part of the secret family recipe," I say, looking mysterious. If Dad can have his buttermilk trick, then I can have my sweet-and-sour trick.

The mom drains her drink quick.

Alone, I eat my pound cake and refill my cup of lemonade to drink in full view of any potential new customers. It's important to show customers that you enjoy your own product. Mr. Fancypants is awake and panting. He seems to have forgotten where he is.

"You're okay, ole guy, you're okay," I tell him as I fill up a bucket of spigot water, which he drinks in huge gulps like he just finished running through a field, instead of waking up from a nap. He finds a pee spot, and then when he's done, he settles back to sleep. He really is a very boring dog.

Cars stop, parents hand me dollars, and kids stir in the sweetness with their free lollipops. When I see Caroline walking over from the house, my hatband is stuffed. There're only three lollipops left in the shoebox, and my lemonade pitcher is empty.

"I know you took a pound cake from the store," she says. "There's crumbs everywhere. Hand over four dollars, Becket. I have an eagle eye on inventory."

Then she plucks four of

my hard-earned dollars out of my hatband in a way that makes me not want to argue it. "Also Nicholas and Zane said your lemonade tasted pretty bad."

We eye the pitcher. There's nothing but melting ice cubes at the bottom.

"They didn't stick around to find out about my many improvements." I lean down to scratch Mr. Fancypants between the ears.

"Like what?"

"A smidge of this, a dash of that. As the saying goes—if at first you don't succeed, try, try again!"

"I wish you'd saved some for me to try."

"Sorry, I succeeded too much. That's why there's none left."

Caroline thinks I'm being mean, but she wasn't the queen of sparkling sweetness when I needed her help finding sugar and honey.

"Another expression is 'I did it my way,'" I call to her back.

And if Gran gives out the lollipops, or I give them—free is free, right? Right?

So why do I feel so sneaky?

CHAPTER 12

Out in the Field

LOOKS LIKE I'M RICH. IN MY COZY BEDROOM, I MOVE MY money—eight smackeroos—from my hatband to my shoebox.

Then I take one dollar out to give to Zane. No more debt for me!

I hide the shoebox all the way in the back of my closet.

Maybe I should do something smart with my earnings. Like buy Noble a magnificent red dog collar with a silver buckle for when he comes home. Or maybe I should get a tiny little camper for Punkin since he's got nowhere to sleep.

Or maybe I should donate it all to an animal shelter?

Because this money, now that I've got it, doesn't feel like sunshine on my face. More like a stormcloud in my head.

Does it really belong to me? Or does it belong to Gran?

I put a checkmark next to "Get Rich Quick" on my list, but I feel strange about it. So I lie on my bed and cover myself with penguins until I hear Dad and Mom pull into the driveway, back from the clinic.

As usual, they are very talkative about what's going on at work, which always sounds like major animal drama. The Peabody Farm calf just got birthed, and

Mrs. Jenkins' best pointer, Dixie, might be going blind.

In all the years I've hung out with my parents, which is pretty much all the same years I've been alive, Mom and Dad never have run out of things to talk about. Sometimes it's the animals, sometimes it's bills or home repairs, sometimes it's us kids—but it's always way more interesting to them than to me. Mom and Dad are more alike than Nicholas and I—and we're twins. It's funny how families work.

There's extra food for lunch on account of Zane the Giant. Each of us has a saucer of chopped-up carrots and apples next to our bowls of pasta. Also, everyone gets a loopy paper straw in our strawberry milk.

"How were your lemonade sales, Becket?" asks Mom with a smile.

"She didn't have enough sugar," says Nicholas.

Dad bops his hand to the side of his head. "How'd we miss that? I'll pick some up later."

"She made it anyway," says Zane. "Unfortunately."

"I used Bee Sweet honey and it was delicious. We're out of honey, too." I hand over my dollar to make Zane be quiet. He pockets it quietly, with a smirk and without a thank you. He and Nicholas tell dumb jokes through the whole lunch. As soon as Dad and Mom leave the kitchen to have grown-ups lunch on the porch, Zane shows Nicholas a lunchroom oldie—how he can take a sip of milk and make it come out of his nose.

"Every weird kid I know does that," I say, "and it's bad for your system."

But then Nicholas makes milk come out of his nose, too. I didn't know he could do that trick. I'm secretly impressed.

"Don't come crying to me when you've destroyed your systems," I tell them.

"Nobody's crying to you. Today is boys against girls day," says Zane.

"There's only one girl," I remind him.

"Fine. Boys against *the* girl." Zane chomps his carrot like it's a cigar.

I know Nicholas feels sorry for me, but since this is his first country play date, he's letting Zane say whatever he wants. Still, I make sure both of them see the annoyedness on my face. If only Frieda were here to be on my team!

After lunch, Nicholas and Zane get fishing lines and nets. "We're gonna catch some sunfish in the pond," Nicholas explains.

"They wriggle and flop like crazy when you bring them up," I tell him. I know Nicholas has never caught a fish in that pond in his life. He looks nervous.

"Let my sister come with us," he suggests to Zane.

Zane looks at me. "You don't seem right for our club," he says.

That gets me feeling spiky. "What do I need to do to get in your club?"

"It's more about what you are already. Do you play a musical instrument?" asks Zane. "Your brother plays the cello, I play saxophone."

"Nope," I say.

"Do you break out in hives or are allergic in some way to more than four things?" asks Zane.

"We're allergic to a lot," explains Nicholas. "Between us, we have allergies to ragweed, strawberries, mold, dust mites—"

"I know all about your allergies, Nicholas, and no, I'm not allergic to any of those things!" I tell them. "Once I thought I was allergic to wool, but I was only itchy."

"Okay, finally—would you do the fire or ice challenge to pledge that *Attack of the Zernoks* is the greatest movie ever made?" asks Nicholas.

"Cause we already did that an hour ago," adds Zane.

"What's the fire or ice challenge?"

"You either drink a spoonful of hot sauce or dump a cup of ice water on your head to show your loyalty that it's the best movie ever!" says Zane like it's so obvious.

"I did ice, Zane did fire," says Nicholas.

"No, thanks," I say. "I'm really not interested in being part of your club. You can keep your three-headed aliens, musical instruments, and hives."

Nicholas's eyes go owly. "If you want to come with us, Becket, you can," he says. I know he'd make it semi-okay for me to be there, but I don't want to squeak along like a fifth wheel on their play date. I wanted my own play date. "Nah," I say.

Zane drops a paw on my brother's shoulder. "Let's go, Nico."

Nico? Nobody calls my brother Nico. I can see in his face he likes it. Did my twin's cool country nickname finally show up?

It isn't until the boys slam outside that I realize Zane took my net.

First I had lemons, then I had lemonade, and now I've got a lonely lemony afternoon stretched ahead. Plus Zane ate all the extra pasta that was supposed to be second helpings for everyone. So I've got some hunger lemons, too.

I go outside and walk through the meadow into the planting fields. A mosquito whines near me. I swat and swat—until I feel a prick near my elbow.

Grrr, she got me!

A fire or ice challenge actually sounds like a fun thing to do. But only with the right kind of friend, like Caleb, who was the best play date ever. Once we made teeny-tiny jellybean and gummy bear pizzas in the toaster oven for our hamblings. Also, Caleb's house had stairs that we could pillow

sled down. At the playground, we both liked mango juice pops from the Yo-Fro health treats truck.

I could really use a mango juice pop right now.

I've sent Caleb two letters to his camp address since we moved. He hasn't sent me back anything.

When I trip and fall over a rock, scraping up my palms, it's almost a relief to stay put, lying on my stomach.

Maybe it is not my destiny to be the Country Goods billboard kid, laughing in the sun. Maybe I'm more of a lone wolf, friendless and pet-free. I close my eyes and take a deep breath . . .

The whistle is loud as a fire siren. I jump up, dizzy.

"Outta the way!" Farmer Jack's tractor is lurching at me like a giant tank.

Did I fall asleep? The sun is in a different place, and my leg has a cramp in it.

I sit up, squinting.

What's going on? That's not Farmer Jack

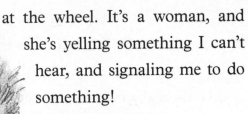

at the wheel. It's a woman, and she's yelling something I can't hear, and signaling me to do something!

"Kid! MOVE!"

"HEY!" When I hear her, I jump to a stand. I can be loud, too. Loud is my specialty. I raise my arms and make my Mrs. Wallerby crossing guard signal for STOP.

Once she's close, the lady puts on the brake.

"You're not Farmer Jack!"

"I'm Farmer Jack's wife, Farmer Jess. And *you* are standing smack in the middle of this field that I'm baling."

I have no idea why tears have started to spill out of my eyes. "I was . . ." It feels like there's a lemon in my throat.

Farmer Jess has

good listening eyes, even if I am not saying much of anything at all. When she takes off her sun-faded blue cap, her curls spring out everywhere. Then she pats the tractor seat. "Jump on."

"On your tractor?"

Farmer Jess smiles. "There isn't anything happening here on Blackberry Farm that's more interesting than what this back-loader can do."

The wheels are higher than my head. "A drastic fall could end it all," I say. "That's a safety tip I learned, back when I lived in the city."

"Good one," says Farmer Jess. "Bend at the knees and jumping's a breeze!"

"I never heard that safety slogan." I wipe my eyes. The slogans are making me feel better already.

"Because I just invented it." Farmer Jess leans down and gives me a hand. I bend my knees, jump, and I'm up! Sitting right next to her.

"When high in the air, take extra care," I say. "I just made that up, too."

"Quick thinker, I like that," says Farmer Jess. "Also, you're safe now. How about just kick back and enjoy the view?"

It's—wow! I can see all the grain fields and the woods. "Beautiful Alert!"

"Beautiful Alert!" repeats Farmer Jess with a smile.

I can't stop looking around. "It's like a farm skyscraper! And now I get to put 'Ride a Tractor' on my Country Kid List!"

"Oh, no. You're not just going to ride this tractor."

"I'm not?"

"You're going to drive it."

"ME?"

"You plus me. We'll team-drive. Don't worry, I'll be right here next to you." Farmer Jess scoots to the side so I'm closer to the wheel. "See what's attached to the back of my tractor?"

I look behind me. "A giant thing-er-a-tor?"

"It's called a round baler. It sweeps up dried bluegrass, rolls it, and nets it into bundles. All morning, I've been making bales up and down these windrows."

I'd seen those huge round wheels of hay on the fields, but I didn't know this thingamajig was making them.

"I can teach you how we kick them out, if you want."

"Yes, I want!"

Farmer Jess shows me how to put my hands on the steering wheel, how to press the button for pickup, when to change to the net-wrap function, and how to use the kicker so that the baler drops a perfect wheel of hay.

It is hot, sweaty, sticky work. But I like it.

"Catch anything yet?" I yell to Nicholas and Zane once we're closer to the pond. I make sure I've got both hands on the wheel, so they can see who is

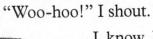 team-driving this back-loader.

"Woo-hoo!" I shout.

I know I look cool in the seat, since Zane stands all the way up. Both boys look like a giant suction-fingered Zernok is about to land on them. Awe and a little bit of fear.

"Hey, guys! Incoming! Watch out for the bluegrass!" I yell as we drop a bale within kicking distance, if anyone could kick something that big.

With two whoops, both boys jump in the pond and start splashing around. I know they're half playing, but also trying to protect themselves from me in my tractor.

"You're a natural, Becket!" calls Farmer Jess, and to prove it, she takes off her red cap and pops it right onto my head.

CHAPTER 13

Dumpster Debt

1. Goodbye, City!
2. Change My Name **to Becket**
3. Do Barnyard Chores ~~(to Get a Country Dog)~~ **and Learn How to Care for Animals**
4. Make a New ~~Best~~ Friend
5. **Get Rich Quick** ✓
6. Drive a Tractor (Like a Natural)

My list looks really good with "Drive a Tractor (Like a Natural)" on it. I'd never have thought of that one till I did it. Too bad Farmer Jess is a grown-up or it could have even counted as a play date.

Which gives me another idea for my list: "Make Something Special."

I think about rearranging my list because this one has to do with number four, but I decide to keep it like it is. There's too much crossing out already. My eyes go right to that scratched-out "best." Now I know some "bests" don't come so easy. It's hard to be best at anything—boat-racer, lemonade-maker, and especially friend-finder. I thought I was okay with Frieda just being my friend. But I don't know if she's even that. Still, I have to do something. If the only kid coming over for play dates is milk-snorting Zane, it's going to be one very long summer.

I push open the squeaky screen door and walk out into the late afternoon. I'm looking for anything that might be a Beautiful Alert. Soon my pockets

are filled with dandelion fluff, odd-shaped twigs, a blue chip of robin's egg, and a pebble as pale and flat as a full moon.

By Sunday night, I've almost forgotten about those lollipops.

Okay, not really. I've been thinking about them pretty nonstop, with a curled-up anxious feeling in my stomach.

At dinnertime, I come inside with a bouquet of goldenrod blooms for our centerpiece. Oops. I spy with my nervous eye: Gran's empty lollipop jar.

Plunk in the middle of the table.

Maybe my best plan is to pretend not to notice it?

"Dee deedle dee," I sing. I set the table. I even remember placemats. I don't make any fuss about asking for cheese cubes in the salad. Instead of picking mushrooms out of the chicken-with-mushrooms dinner, I spit them neatly from my mouth into my napkin.

Nobody is talking at all about the lollipop jar.

After dinner, Gran yawns and says she is turning in early. Nicholas scoops bowls of chocolate chip ice cream for everyone. I clear plates and put them in the dishwasher. "Dum dee dum," I sing. "Dee dum dee. I think I'll turn in early, too. Gotta rest up for camp. Goodnight, everybody."

I am on the first step when Dad calls out, "Rebecca Branch?"

Becket, Dad. But now's not the time. "Yep?"

"Could you come back and sit down here at the table with Mom and me? Just for a minute?"

Oh, boy. I really don't want to come back and sit down. Not even for a minute.

I come back. I sit down.

"You never told us how much money you made from your lemonade stand yesterday," says Mom.

First I take off my glasses and clean them with

the edge of my T-shirt. Then I put them back on. "Eight dollars, minus the dollar I owed Zane."

"Becket," says Mom. "Did you give out all of Gran's special barley-sugar lollipops so that customers would buy your lemonade?"

"Yes." I squirm. "I thought they were free to give away. Since that's what Gran does."

"So do you think they're free for Gran to give away? Or free for you to give away?" asks Mom.

"I'm confused about that question," I say.

"Then you should have asked," says Dad. "If you never ask, you'll never know."

Mom takes one of my hands and folds it like a hand sandwich between hers. She looks into my eyes. "You need to pay back Gran. Did you know that one bag of barley lollipops is nine dollars?"

It is safe to say that I did not know that.

"You need to give Gran all the profits you made from the lemonade stand, and then you only owe her a couple of dollars," says Dad.

"*Owe?*" I wonder if Gran turned in early so she didn't have to see me get so squirmy. "Do you mean I'm in *debt?*"

"It's only fair that you pay for those lollipops," says Mom.

"*How?*" I ask. "There's hardly any ways in the world for a kid to make money."

Dad nods. "That's why we were thinking you can take over one of the jobs around the house."

"But I'm already taking care of the animals. That's a lot."

"Helping out is what family is all about. Nicholas is in charge of unloading the dishwasher every morning, and he has to fold all the laundry. Caroline helps out at the store. And yes, you have shown great responsibility with the animals," says

Dad. "But now you need to repay this small debt, and Mom and I want to help. So we thought we'd give you a paying chore, of fifty cents every time you take the trash bag to the dumpster," he says. "Just four nights, starting tonight."

I look over at the bag slumped by the kitchen door.

Big, white, heavy, smelly.

The dumpster is by the store. That's two whole city blocks away. That's not even one subway or bus stop, but it feels like a long way to lug trash.

"Okay," I say. "But just so you know, I wasn't going to spend the lemonade money on myself. Since Punkin has no home, I was getting him a camper."

Mom and Dad don't seem too impressed by my thoughtfulness.

Then Dad points to the bag. "It can't take itself out."

When I pick it up—oof! "It feels like there's a

seventeen-pound frozen turkey in here! I'll have to carry my fireproof safety pocket flashlight between my teeth!"

"We have faith in you," says Mom. "We'll be right here."

"If you see a coyote, run," Caroline calls from the family room. I know that this is the new, slightly meaner and more teasing Country Caroline, and I shouldn't pay her any attention. But it gives me scary in-the-dark thoughts anyway.

Farm dark is darker than city dark. No streetlights. No neighbor windows. In the city, you have Stranger Danger, but out here you get a shivery feeling of All Alone With Wild Animals Danger.

If only Noble were at my side, guiding my way.

When I drag the bag, it makes an eely, slithering sound behind me.

The woods aren't close. But what if a bear can sniff this garbage?

Bears will brave anything for a snack, and what makes a better snack than a sixty-three-pound kid?

I'm halfway to the dumpster and my teeth are starting to hurt from biting my flashlight when I hear a whole lot of noise from the henhouse.

What the . . . ? I drop my bag.

Are the chickens always this loud at night?

I listen harder.

Archie's the loudest. I'd recognize his honking and quacking anywhere. And that ole duck doesn't sound right. His noises are too panicked. Even the squawking chickens can't drown him out.

"EMERGENCY!" I yell as loud as I can.

"SOMEBODY CALL 911! THERE'S TROUBLE AT THE HENHOUSE, PEOPLE!"

But nobody can hear me. I'm too far from the house. I've got to think on my feet, but my feet aren't quick enough to run me back to the house for help. This is a right-this-second problem—and it's up to me to do something!

I aim my flashlight, sprint over to the henhouse, fling open the door, and—

"OH, NOOOO!"

CHAPTER 14

Intruder!

I BEAM MY LIGHT INTO A PAIR OF GLINTING EYES.

He's not a big raccoon. He's even smaller than a medium-sized raccoon.

Growing up with vets, I've been warned to watch out for critters with rabies—how they act snappish and restless and bite on themselves. This little bandit just looks scared. He's been interrupted in the middle of his crime, with an egg in his paws.

Do I move? Do I freeze?

At least he's close to the screen he must have torn to get in here.

All I want him to do is go.

That's probably all he wants, too.

The thing is, he won't. It's like he can't. We're both superglued to our spots.

Meantime, it's a madhouse in this henhouse. Poor Archie keeps honking and running around in a circle with his head down and his wings spread. The chickens are flapping and squawking. It feels a little bit like being back on a city playground when someone gets hit by a shovel or falls off the monkey bars, and all the rest of the kids try to tell one single babysitter at the same time.

"Calm down," I say to the chickens in a babysitter voice, even though my heart is beating overtime. "Safety first—because injuries last."

The raccoon's nose twitches the air. Maybe he's trying to figure out how to grab a chicken dinner for takeout.

He better not be. But raccoons are wily. This one looks like he might do anything. After all, he's already got an egg.

Argh! "Catch a Raccoon by Surprise" was never on my list.

We are locked in a stare-off. Then—*zzzwwwp*—the raccoon is gone. Ducking out of the henhouse at the same moment Dad and Caroline rush in to meet me.

"Was that a RACCOON? *Eeeeeeeeee!*" Caroline shrieks as her head whips around.

"What happened?" asks Dad. "Are you okay? Did the raccoon come at you?"

"I'm fine, the chickens are fine, but . . ." My eyes blink with tears as I point to Archie. He's got his wing scooped up over his head as he hops in a hurt, bewildered circle.

Dad sweeps down and tucks Archie in a firm hold so that he can inspect his face.

"What happened to him?" asks Caroline.

"It's Archie's eye," says Dad. "Looks like the raccoon gouged it."

Noooo, poor Arch! A gouged eye is as opposite as I can think of a Beautiful Alert.

"Does *gouged* mean gone?" squeaks Nicholas, who's right behind with Mom and Gran.

"In this case, yes." Dad frowns, grim. "Mom and I better run Arch over to the clinic to clean him up and dress this wound." He looks at me. "Think you can calm down these chickens?"

"No problem." Even though my heart is aching for Archie and racing from my raccoon run-in, it also feels pretty good that Dad is talking to me like I'm the leader—probably since I'm the one who gathers the eggs every morning.

After Mom and Dad leave with poor injured Archie, I show Gran the rip in the screen where the raccoon tore through. Together, we patch it with duct tape. "This'll hold until tomorrow, when we can secure it with a stronger welded-wire," she says. "Raccoons and foxes in the henhouse are a farmer's worst worry."

Laying Godiva is staring at me from her roost.

"What's wrong?" I ask her. "I just saved you from being raccoon dinner! You should be thanking me."

That old hen just ruffles her feathers.

"Okay, I might not be your favorite, but I bet you'd pick me any day over that bandit egg raider." I take one step closer, and I try out that *tsk tsk* sound that Gran uses.

She looks back at me like *yes, I know that cluck.* Is it a comfort to her? "We've all had a fright," I tell her. "I might not have looked scared, but I was. A little. Now I'm not. Everything's okay now."

I stay behind with Godiva and the rest of the rattled chickens to make sure they feel loved and settled. I sprinkle chicken snacks, sunflower seeds, and stale bread crumble for them to hunt and peck. I don't leave until all of the chickens are comfortably roosting together.

Back at the house, Gran is making people snacks—toast with cinnamon butter, along with peppermint herb tea. We sit together at the table as we wait for everyone to come home from the clinic.

When Mom and Dad bring in Archie, he's got a patch over his missing eye.

"Arrr, it's Cap'n Quacky," jokes Caroline.

But I'm worried. "Will Archie be okay living his life as a one-eyed duck?"

"He'll be fine," assures Mom. "He's one lucky duck. Raccoons can be outright vicious, especially when they're caught off guard. Good thing that one was a teenager. Becket, you were in a serious situation. If that raccoon had been any bigger, he might have held his ground."

I try not to feel too thrilled, but after all of my

danger warnings—to myself and to everybody else—it finally happened. I Survived Serious Country Danger!

"Since I saved all the chickens, I probably don't have to carry trash to the dumpster this week, right?"

"Wrong," says Dad.

"Nice try, though, sweetie," says Mom.

I shrug. "If you never ask, you'll never know."

CHAPTER 15

Fair Weather

"THE FAIRS ARE COMING! THE FAIRS ARE COMING!" I'VE BEEN cheering my cheer at Young Explorers ever since I found out about their visit. Some of the campers got super-excited about my news, until Counselor Pete asked me to explain that it's the Fairs, our friends, who are coming from the city to celebrate Caroline's birthday. Not fairs with bumper cars and cotton candy, which was what everyone was thinking.

"It's kind of like you're tricking us, Becket," says Cadie in a snippy voice.

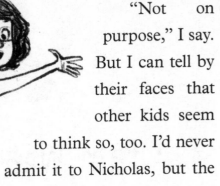

"Not on purpose," I say. But I can tell by their faces that other kids seem to think so, too. I'd never admit it to Nicholas, but the 3B section has been hard. Camp Easy Breeze had loved my loud camp spirit, but it hasn't worked the same way with Young Explorers. This camp has been a bran muffin amount of fun, not a banana split with three cherries and sprinkles amount of fun.

So I'm doubly excited to see some old friends.

"I'm so excited for the Fairs," I say at breakfast.

"You keep saying that," says Nicholas.

"I've said it before, and I'll say it again."

"According to the *Farmers' Almanac*, this weekend will be the hottest weather of the summer," says Dad.

"I hope the Fairs can take the heat." Caroline bites her lip.

"We've got a pond for cooling off, and a freezer full of ice cream," I remind her.

"Annabelle doesn't like to swim," says Caroline. "We took lessons at the Y back in kindergarten. She got swimmer's ear even before she went in the water."

"There's other stuff to do," I say. "You know she's gonna love it!"

"I doubt it," says Caroline. "Annabelle isn't some country bumpkin, like us!"

"I only wanted to help," I snap back. "And stop calling us bumpkins! I looked it up and it means an unsophisticated, socially awkward person from the countryside. I might be from the countryside, but I'm none of those other things."

"Me either," says Nicholas. "I'm social! I've got more friends here than I did in the city!"

"Okay, kids," says Mom. "I'd love us to all pull together to make this weekend a success. How about it?"

Caroline shrugs and chews her toast.

"Are the Fairs bringing Frankie?" asks

Nicholas. Frankie Fair is Annabelle's four-year-old brother, who is a freckled fireball of pure crazy.

"Of course they'll bring Frankie," says Caroline, right back to snapping. "Where else would he go?"

"An orphanage or a kennel?" suggests Nicholas. "In the city, I could escape him. But there's no good place to hide from Frankie here."

"He'll be sharing your room, too, Nicholas," I point out. "But you're more social now, so it shouldn't be a problem."

Nicholas looks sick. He goes upstairs. A minute later, we hear his new cello tune, probably called "I Will Never Survive a Weekend of Frankie," floating down to us.

Then it's the end of the week, and the day of the Fairs. Gran extra-weeds her garden, including the front-door sunflowers. Dad bakes his banana loaf bread. Caroline brews a pitcher of iced tea.

Mom drives to town to pick up a bakery cake.

A store-bought cake is Caroline's birthday wish. "Just because we're country you-know-whats doesn't mean we need *everything* homemade," she says. "Everyone likes bakery cakes."

I'm sure Caroline is mostly thinking about what Annabelle likes.

"What a birthday girl wants, a birthday girl gets—that's the rule!" I say. I don't want anyone to forget this incredibly important rule when it's October, and my birthday.

Nicholas thumbs-ups me, since that's his birthday, too.

That afternoon, we wait on the porch—even Mr. Fancypants, who I brought outside specially so he doesn't miss a thing. We switched over from using Bee Sweet honey to hiding his pills in peanut butter. Mr. Fancypants loves that taste even more. Unfortunately, there's usually a peanut butterish smell on my hands, and I think that's why he's started napping in my lap. Even though Mr. Fancypants is gassy and heavy it's not the worst, to feel him breathing calm, and to know that my lap is as comfy for him as his arthritis pillow.

I see the car before everyone else. "They're heeeeeeeere!" I call, even if I can't move fast from the dog weight on me.

Annabelle's mom hops out with a big whoop and hugs. She gives Mom and Dad a gift box from Sugarman's Deli. When I finally get Mr. Fancypants relocated and join up to check it out, I see that it's filled with our favorite crackers, pickles, and mustards. Meantime, Frankie is madly turning somersaults across the grass while hollering, "Look how many I can do in a row! Nicholas, count!"

Annabelle's dad starts to unload bags from the trunk.

"Hi, Annabelle." Caroline peers through the car window.

"I'll be with you in a sec. I'm still feeling a

little car sick." When Annabelle climbs out of the car, she's wearing her usual black jeans and black shirt and black boots and she looks wobbly. But she gives Caroline a squeeze and a wrapped birthday present that turns out to be a silver-framed picture of Caroline and Annabelle with their other best friends, Lester, Jules, and Alex, all arm-in-arm walking down our old street.

"Thank you." Caroline stares for a long time at the picture. "I can't believe I won't see any of you at school this year." Her eyes fill up.

As cranky as Caroline has been toward me lately, I have to give Annabelle a frown for bringing my sister a present that makes her so sad and homesick.

"Finished my cartwheels!" shouts Frankie. "How many did I do, Nicholas?"

"Frankie, who drew that mustache on your upper lip?" I ask him.

"I did it myself! It's a bad-guy mustache," says Frankie. "You can tell because it curls down, not up, on the ends. Hey, Nicholas, check out these babies." He makes arm muscles. "Also I can swim with no floaties. Also I've got night vision. Also carrots still make me throw up because I've got like two thousand tastebugs. Other things that make me throw up are cauliflower, beans, avocados, and peaches."

Nicholas looks at me with owl eyes.

"Do you want to see my room?" Caroline asks

Annabelle. "I don't have to share with my little sister anymore."

"No, thanks. I don't want to go inside," says Annabelle. "I've been stuck in that car for hours." She makes being stuck in a car sound like Caroline's fault.

"How about a farm tour?" I shout. "First stop, the swing."

"I can swing until forever!" yells Frankie. I already know this is true. That's why I suggested it. Nicholas and I give Frankie pushes until our arms wear out, while Annabelle and Caroline stand apart and watch.

Annabelle keeps slapping herself.

"Want a turn?" asks Caroline.

"No, thanks." Annabelle slaps. "There's tons of bugs out here. Can't we go somewhere less terrible?"

Caroline looks worried. There's no escaping bugs on a farm.

"I've got this," I say, digging into my back pocket for my little tin of Udderly Useful balm. It's an old-timey farmer remedy for soothing chafed cow udders, but Gran says it works for just about anything chapped or dry. I use it on Pickle and Chew when their hooves look cracked, and I also use it on my own lips. "Keeps the bugs away," I say. Which might be true. It's got a slightly medicine smell.

"Relief." Annabelle dips her fingers and rubs it on her arms and chest and face. "Ah, already better. What is this stuff?"

Caroline knows what my balm is, and we

exchange a look of slight terror. Annabelle won't be happy to know that she's rubbed cow ChapStick all over her skin.

"Just a boring bug balm. I know, let's get a snack!" I clap my hands together. "Next stop, the berry patch! I think that's less buggy."

At the berry patch, the first thing I see is a bug. At least it's only a tiny green inchworm scooting up and down across a dandelion leaf. I pick the leaf to show Annabelle. "So cute, right? Not all bugs are bad. You can't go wrong with an inchworm."

"Bugs. No, thanks." Annabelle doesn't even look at it.

Frankie stuffs raspberries in his mouth until he's got chipmunk cheeks. Annabelle picks a single raspberry and sniffs it. "Are these okay to eat? They haven't been cleaned like the ones from Country Goods Farm Markets."

"Actually, Country Goods Farm raspberries come from all the way up in Vermont," says Caroline. "A berry from our patch is always better than fruit from far away, which can get bruised or moldy and gross on the truck."

Caroline has learned a lot from working at Branch's—but I didn't know that Country Goods Farm was so far away! Suddenly the land of Noble feels more like an imaginary place, or a dream.

Annabelle doesn't look like she believes what Caroline has said. I watch her let the berry drop from her fingers to the grass.

"I'm bursting berry goodness!" says Frankie. He does a couple of somersaults. When he comes upright, he looks woozy. "Better give my stomach a time-out."

"Let me show you the henhouse," I tell the Fairs. "Come on."

As soon as we walk in, the chickens greet us with their usual clucking. It's only Godiva who starts ruffling her annoyance at having visitors. "That hen despises everyone," says Nicholas. "She's our gran's prize, but she's sooo cranky. Don't go near her!"

Annabelle squeals with alarm. "What are we even doing here?" she asks. "No, thanks! This whole farm is a danger zone."

Caroline looks upset. She likes to come in here sometimes to feed the hens treats, and we both think their pecking and clucking is funny. I wonder if this is her last straw with Miss Annabelle "No, Thanks" Fair.

"We should go," says Caroline.

I take a very deep breath. Then I scoop up Godiva in my best firm Gran style. "Godiva's cluck is worse than her peck." I wait to be pecked, but Godiva just rests in the crook of my arm. I can actually feel her settling in and calming down in my snug arms. Caroline and Nicholas look impressed. "She's nothing to worry about, see? It's the raccoons that give us trouble. Last month, a raccoon broke in and attacked poor old Arch."

Annabelle shivers. "It's like, how do you do it? Critters are hiding everywhere! Aren't you scared of bears?"

Caroline bursts out laughing, but it's one of those hard, mad laughs. "Jeez, Annabelle! Were you always this much of a fraidy-cat?"

Annabelle goes silent.

"His eye is mostly healed now," I say quietly.

"It kinda looks cool," says Frankie. "It makes him look like he's always winking."

"No, it's gross," Annabelle says.

She doesn't want to visit Pickle and Chew, either.

Even when I offer to show how I've been exercising them.

"They're gentle old folks," I tell her. "You could ride one, if you want."

But Annabelle doesn't want to be talked into it.

"Oh, I know! Let's check out the swarming," says Caroline. "It's pretty dramatic."

"Annabelle won't like the swarming," mutters Nicholas at my side as we walk over to the apple orchard. "Maybe Caroline's had it, and she's trying to scare her."

"Yeah, or maybe she's just stopped caring."

When Annabelle sees that a swarming means thousands of honeybees huddled in the hollow of an apple tree, so close together they look like a nestled pinecone, she backs off super fast. It's the biggest "No, Thanks" we showed her yet.

"People can die getting too close to bee hives!" Annabelle reminds us.

"That's why you need a fun safety tip, like *bee careful*," I tell her. "And it's not a hive, it's a swarm. The workers make a bee cluster, while scouts look for a new location for their queen—and *that* location will be their hive."

"They won't sting unless you get close enough to bother them," says Nicholas.

No surprise, Annabelle has already moved far away. There's nothing she likes about Blackberry Farm. She doesn't want to race garter snakes or catch frogs and salamanders. She doesn't want to pick sour summer apples or even go swimming, although it's so hot, our clothes are sticking to our skin.

"Annabelle didn't bring a bathing suit," says Frankie. "No way will she swim in a dirty farm pond."

"There's nothing to be afraid of, Annabelle," I tell her. "It's just some sunfish and turtles in there."

"I'm not scared of ponds or turtles." But Annabelle's voice lifts up on its way to the end of that sentence. When we all go to the pond for a family swim, she stays on the bank and watches.

"Who knew Annabelle Fair would turn out to be the kid version of Mr. Fancypants?" says Nicholas in my ear. "She's the way I used to be a long time ago, when we first moved here." He looks proud to say it.

"Yeah, totally. She's scared of everything," I say. "Even Mr. Fancypants is braver than Annabelle about country life." And later when I give him his second peanut butter–covered heart pill before dinner, I tell him so.

CHAPTER 16

Midnight Guest

IT LOOKS LIKE RAIN AS WE SETTLE AROUND THE PORCH table for Caroline's birthday dinner. I enjoy seeing so much of this dark, clouding-over sky at once. In the city, you only see chunks of sky between the buildings. Here, the weather is everywhere.

"Woooo-eeee, the *Almanac* sure didn't predict this one," says Dad.

"Neither did the local news or my weather app," says Mr. Fair. He leans back contentedly. "Nothing like watching a summer storm."

"As long as there's no lightning," says Annabelle.

Lightning spears across the sky. Annabelle shivers.

I count slowly. "One Mississippi, two Mississippi, three Missis—"

Thunder booms.

"The storm's half a mile away," says Caroline.

"What? I don't get it," says Annabelle.

"After you see lightning, you count the number of seconds before the thunder," I explain. "Every five seconds is a mile."

"Oh," says Annabelle. "That's cool."

Caroline smiles at me faintly. It's the first time Annabelle has decided that anything about today was cool.

"Go, thunderstorm!" says Frankie. Half of his bad-guy mustache has rubbed off, which makes him look extra nuts. "Knock knock, who's there?

THUNDERSTORM! I hope the house isn't split in half by lightning, that'd be bad!"

"Stop it, Frankie, you pest," says Annabelle, but she looks worried again.

Luckily, the storm is more of a spattering, but even when it's over, the clouds decide to stick around. Dinner is all of Caroline's favorites: twisty three-color pasta salad, garden salad, and fruit salad. Caroline never met a salad she didn't like.

After dinner come presents.

Mom and Dad give Caroline a necklace with a letter C charm. The Fairs give her a cute purple suitcase on wheels. "For visiting me on *my* birthday!" says Annabelle.

Frankie gives Caroline a rock that he took from our driveway, but he pretends that's not true. "I found it lasterday on our block, by the hot dog cart!" he insists.

I give Caroline a belt that I latch-hooked during crafts time at Young Explorers.

Nicholas brings down Clive and plays "Happy Birthday." Cello music can turn even a happy tune into something that makes me picture a lonely winter road, but Caroline loves it.

Finally, Mom and Dad walk out the red velvet cake with twelve lit rainbow candles and a sparkler candle to grow on. Right as Caroline blows out her candles, the storm sneaks in again. Drops of rain begin plopping softly onto the porch roof, and then—*boom!*—it's really here.

"Avalanche!" calls Frankie. "Volcano! Blizzard!" When lightning zigzags across the sky, Frankie is the first inside. Nicholas gets the hiccups and follows, Annabelle right on his tail. Nicholas and Annabelle definitely tie for being storm scaredy cats. Not that I would point it out to him, since Nicholas is feeling so good about other ways he's become brave.

In the next minute, the rain hammers slantwise. Winds kick up and begin blowing our party hats and napkins onto the field. The rest of us rush indoors. Everyone is laughing, even after the lights flicker off and we are plunged into darkness.

"I bet a tree fell and brought down a power line," says Dad. "We could be without electricity all night."

"Good thing it's bedtime," says Mom. She lights the hurricane lamps so that we can find our way to our rooms.

"I don't like this," mumbles Nicholas.

"I REALLY don't like this!" shrieks Annabelle.

"When the power goes out, please don't shout," I tell her.

With only the wobbly lamplight to guide us, we file upstairs. Annabelle is gripping tight to Caroline, and Frankie is gripping tight to Nicholas, while Mr. Fancypants and I bring up the rear. I can feel Mr. F trembling like a fat, scared football in my arms.

Everyone gets a sleep buddy—except me.

In my bed, I am wide-awake, staring at the ceiling. I listen to the rain pound on the roof. *Crrraaaack!* Lightning brightens my room and turns my face erasers into tiny mean-eyed goblins. My heart is racing too fast to sleep.

In the city when it rained, I always had Caroline in the bed right next to me. She used to make my penguins sing silly songs like: "It's fine in here, we have no fear. Outside's the storm, inside's the warm." Also the streetlights stayed on even when the electricity went off. So I never thought to be scared about thunderstorms. "When the power goes out, please don't pout," I whisper to myself on repeat.

Not every single thing about the country is better than the city.

The storms are definitely scarier.

I burrow deeper under my quilt. It is hard work being brave.

Creeeeeeeak!

"Hello?" I sit straight up like a vampire. Who is opening my bedroom door? There's no one there! A snorfling noise near the floor makes me look down. "Oh! Mr. Fancypants!"

He shuffles in at his usual extremely slow pace. I had no idea he even knew where my bedroom was. It must have taken him a million years to get down the hall. It's not a trip he makes too often.

"What are you doing here?" I whisper. I scoot out of bed and give him a pat, then hurry to get him some water in the bathroom, using my own drinking cup. He slurps for a long time. It's a little gross but there's nothing else. Then I scoop him up and lift him onto my bed. His heart is beating faster than mine. At the next crack of lightning, he licks my face. *Oof*, Mr. Fancypants has some really bad old-dog breath. But he sure is scared.

"Okay, looks like you can be my bunkmate tonight, Mr. F," I tell him. "Just calm down that old heart of yours." I give him his special ear scratches. I wonder if Mr. Fancypants also thinks country storms are scarier than city ones.

When I'd written "Host the Fairs" as the next thing on my list, I hadn't thought I'd also be hosting Mr. F, too. Then again, Mr. Fancypants has never chosen me over Nicholas before. Maybe he knows that I'm not as bothered by lightning? Or that I won't hold on to him too tight, the way Nicholas does? It takes Mr. Fancypants a long time to get himself comfy. He scuffles at the covers, then he has another coughing fit, then he starts up his panting again, and then I have to get him more water. Some of it spills on my pajamas, ugh.

Just when I think I'm going to be awake all night with him, Mr. Fancypants makes one last *hrrrmph*, curls up at the end of my bed, and falls into a very deep sleep. He makes a nice warm lump at my feet, and his snoring is so loud that it even drowns out the sound of the rain.

CHAPTER 17

Make Something Special

THE NEXT MORNING AFTER BREAKFAST, THE FAIRS SAY goodbye. After they're gone, and with the weekend over, Caroline is in a slump of missing Annabelle.

"Even if Annabelle didn't have the greatest time, I know you tried to help," she says to me.

"No problem," I say. "I wish she'd liked the country better." I brace myself for the usual bumpkin comment.

"She didn't give it a chance," says Caroline. "It's too bad she doesn't have your good eye for Beautiful Alerts." She smiles at me for a moment, a real, from-her-heart smile that makes me feel like we are sisters again.

"Remember, it's only thirty-eight days until you can go to the city for Annabelle's birthday," says Mom. "That'll be fun."

"And you'll get to use your new wheelie suitcase," says Dad.

"It's fun to look forward to something," says Mom.

"When you start school, you'll make some brand-new friends, too, don't forget," says Dad.

"It's been a quiet summer for you, Caroline," says Mom.

"Hey, it's been a quiet summer for me, too," I

remind them. "The only thing that's been noisy about it is the fact that I'm noisy."

Mom and Dad laugh, but I'm not really joking.

Meanwhile, Caroline goes back to drooping around the house like a flower without water.

That afternoon, the mail comes with—a postcard from Caleb!

Dear Becket,

Camp is fun. Your letter was funny! I like your new name.

I traded my toothbrush for some socks.

We almost won on Flag Day but our canoe tipped over.

From,

Caleb

Even though I'm so happy to hear from Caleb, it gives me that pain of missing him that I haven't had since the start of summer.

I take out my list to look at it again. I've got a little more work to do on "Make Something Special." I guess I thought it would be easy to make new friends because I'd always had my old friends, so I never had to put in the extra effort. Live and learn, as practically every grown-up I ever met likes to say. I get out my shoebox of Beautiful Alerts for some final touches.

When I'm done, it looks pretty good. I made the wrapping paper last week, a penguin pattern, and once it's all taped up, I tie it with the long blue ribbon I saved from Caroline's birthday cake box.

After I put away my project, I'm still in an art mood, so I add a sketch of Mr. Fancypants to the bottom of my Country Kid List page, sitting like a chunk on his cushion, right next to Noble. Even though Noble looks cool, my sketch of Mr. Fancypants has many more realistic details. I work on it a long time, so that I even get his bulgy eyes and his jowls just right.

Then I put a bunch of exclamation marks next to "Drive a Tractor (Like a Natural)" because I want to remember the excitement of being up high near the blue sky, behind the wheel and on the move. I should always be on the lookout for how good that felt.

The next morning after Nicholas and I are dropped off at Young Explorers, I've got my package ready. I see Frieda on the front lawn. She is playing Frisbee with some of the older kids. Dang, Frieda is great at Frisbee. Plus she knows how to be friends with anyone, even older kids I'd be nervous to talk to.

I stand on the sidelines, and once there's a break in the game, Frieda runs over. "What's up?"

"Here," I say.

"Oh." Frieda turns over the package in her hands. "Homemade wrapping paper? These penguins are too cute."

"You can open it whenever," I add. "Like, later. Maybe when you're home."

"Okay," she says. But then she pulls the ribbon and unwraps the paper right in front of me.

"Wow." She holds the boat up to inspect every single detail. "You made this—for me?"

"As a replacement, yep."

"But that boat took me an hour to make. This one must have taken—"

"A few weeks," I finish. "I worked on it every night. I sanded it and painted

all the detail myself. I made the Frieda out of a matchstick and her dress out of dandelion fluff. It's shiny because I put two coats of glaze on it. Gran helped me stitch the canvas for the sail."

"That's really nice of you, Becket," says Frieda. "It was never a big deal that you sank the first one." But then she looks me in the eye. "When I first met you, I thought maybe you were sort of a braggy loudmouth," she admits. "But you've definitely chilled out. You're a good sharer at crafts time, and the stories you tell about Laying Godiva and Archie and Pickle and Chew make all the kids laugh."

A braggy loudmouth? How awful. "I'm glad you like my stories, but I promise, Frieda, I can be a quietmouth, too."

She smiles. "Cool. This was really thoughtful of you. I can't wait to launch the new FF *Frieda-tastic* when I get home. We have a little pond, so it can't disappear downstream."

I smile so big that the feeling stays with me through crafts time, where I try to be an even better sharer. At lunch, I tell the story of how Mr. Fancypants sneaked into my room to snore out the thunderstorm. Kids do laugh! Nothing works better than a nice compliment to make you want to prove that it's true.

That evening in the middle of dinner, Mom's cell phone rings.

"Here we go," says Dad, thinking it's a vet emergency, but soon Mom looks pleased and is nodding. "How nice. Thank you," she says. "I think this will be a yes. Sure, let's put the girls on."

Then Mom hands the phone—to me. I am already smiling, because I have a feeling I know who it is.

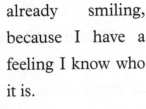

"Hi, Becket," says Frieda in a happy voice. "I tried out my new boat! When I asked my parents if you could come over to watch me sail it, they thought it would be fun to have a whole family play date. And Nicholas can come, too."

"Yeah! We're on!" calls Nicholas, who has overheard everything from across the table.

"Cool," I say. I push past the twinge of not

wanting to share Frieda with Nicholas. "We'd love to."

"Also, will you bring Mr. Fancypants so he can meet Oro?"

"Oh, sure." Frieda sounds so enthusiastic and hopeful, I just don't have the heart to tell her that the most amazing thing about Mr. F is how he sleeps every single hour of the day, except for the hour that he's eating.

The Franca family play date has even got Caroline out of her droop. "I've been wanting to see those alpacas all summer!" she says once I get off the call.

"We'll need to bring Mr. Fancypants's arthritis cushion, and we should give him his muscle relaxer an hour before we leave," I instruct. "Otherwise, he'll feel all the bumps on the car ride."

Mr. F, who is right at my feet, looks at me like he is glad I suggested all these things. "It'll be okay, Mr. F," I tell him. "I've got your back."

CHAPTER 18

Runaway Suki

SATURDAY, AS WE TURN UP THE FRANCAS' DRIVEWAY LINED with big shaggy pine trees, we see a sign with the outline shape of an alpaca.

"Alpaca Crossing!" I look both ways. "When alpacas are around, you'd better slow down. But I don't see any—clear to move, Dad!"

As we pull close to the farmhouse, Oro bounds over to greet us. He's bigger from the last time I saw him, but he is still a happy golden ball of puppy fun.

When I put Mr. Fancypants on the ground, he sniffs around and seems very interested in his new surroundings. Oro tries to get him to play, but when he realizes it's not going to happen, he bounds off.

"Mr. F is a senior citizen," I explain to Frieda, who looks a little disappointed, but what can I do? That's how Mr. F rolls—ancient and wheezy.

Frieda's family has arranged a picnic table lunch under a tree, which is a sweet spot for me to place Mr. F on his cushion, right on time for his nap. The table is full of things to eat. Frieda's mom introduces us to the whole Franca family—there's some cousins and aunts and uncles, and too many names to keep track of, though I do try—and then she tells us each dish. I heap my plate with little rolls called *papas rellenas*.

"That's potato dough stuffed with hard-boiled eggs and raisins, then baked. Sometimes we add meat," explains Frieda's mom. "And we make the dough from our own potato crop." I eat two *papas rellenas*, and I kick Nicholas under the picnic table when he reaches for his seventh.

There is also a spicy, smoky roast chicken, *pollo a la brasa*, and a custard called *tres leches* for dessert.

"Whenever I think I should stop eating, my stomach finds more space!" says Nicholas.

Dad laughs. "I think that's a problem for us all," he says.

Not me. I've still got a case of nerves for this play date to work out, and I don't want to mess anything up. At least Frieda still likes her boat, which she passes around the table for everyone to check out.

While the grown-ups have coffee, Frieda's dad sends us to feed the alpacas. Outside the barn, Frieda and her older sister, Daisy, fill some flat metal feed pans. When they start shaking the pans, the food makes that loud, sliding sound that is music to animals' furry ears.

And suddenly, here they are! Loping up from the pasture all in a herd. The alpacas know that noise means their dinner is served. Their long slender necks and perky faces are even cuter in person.

Caroline gasps in delight. "Oh, my gosh." Her eyes are shiny. "These are the sweetest-looking animals I have ever seen!"

The alpacas are all different colors—white, cream, sandy, and black. They make noises like soft kazoos.

"We have seventeen alpacas altogether," says Frieda. "Half the land is for them to graze, and the other half is for our potatoes and corn crops. Here, hold the pans, so you can feed them yourselves."

Caroline has a lot of cash register experience this

summer, but not much animal feeding experience. She holds the pan with straight-out arms and keeps taking a step back so the alpacas can't get close enough to eat. And there is *no way* Nicholas will feed the alpacas. He is really not enjoying this.

"I've been taking care of our donkey and mule this summer," I tell Frieda, trying not to sound loud and braggy. "They like to have constant shade and water. They get uncomfortable when it's too hot, so I try to exercise them either early in the morning or after dinner."

"Same with alpacas!" says Frieda. "I'm the one who feeds them and looks after them. Daisy prefers to garden."

"I like gardens, too," says Caroline. "Mostly to make salads."

"Me too," says Daisy. "I made the one you had at lunch."

"I had three helpings. I need that recipe," says Caroline.

"It's just lettuce plus everything," says Daisy, and both girls crack up.

The alpacas make happy humming and crunching sounds. Out of the corner of my eye, I see Nicholas inching his way to the paddock gates. I think I'm the only one noticing until I hear Frieda say, "Nicholas, don't open that!"

Too late. Just as Nicholas swings open the gate to slip through and escape, a chocolate-brown alpaca also charges through it.

"No, Suki!" Frieda claps her hands and whistles. "She's our new girl—the wild one. Come back, Soooo!" She unhooks a thin nylon halter from a nail outside the barn and looks at me. "Want to help me chase down an alpaca?"

The answer to that is YES. I scoop a handful of pellets for my pockets, and we start chasing Suki, who is bounding across the fields.

She's faster than we are, but we never lose sight.

Running through the open pasture with the wind on my face is a Beautiful Alert on the inside.

When we finally catch up with Suki, she's resting under a shady tree.

"She's cushed," says Frieda. "That's another word for lying down with her legs folded underneath. It means she feels relaxed."

"I'll feed her to distract her while you harness," I say.

Frieda nods. "Good plan."

I creep up with my palms open wide to offer Suki some pellets. She puts her mouth on my palm and crunches away as Frieda slips on the halter.

"You're smart with animals," says Frieda.

"So are you."

We smile at each other.

We get Suki to stand, and then we walk on either side of her back to the barn. Frieda holds the lead. "Suki just got here last month, and she's still skittish," Frieda says. "It's hard for her, being new."

"It's hard for me to be new, too," I blurt. "I'm

nervous about school next month. Nicholas is already good friends with Zane, and you make friends with everyone so easily."

"But you're so outgoing, Becket. I never think you get nervous," says Frieda. When I don't say anything, she looks thoughtful. "I guess outgoing people can be shy, too."

"YEP!" I agree, shyly.

Frieda laughs. Then she presses my nose freckle. "I've been wanting to do that forever."

"It's fine," I tell her. "Everyone does. I'm used to it."

After we pen Suki, we rejoin the grown-ups. Mr. Fancypants is shuffling around and around in a circle. He is having a hard time finding his comfort zone. I end up putting him on my lap, and then just hanging out with him while he naps as the others play a game of Frisbee with Oro. Daisy and Frieda are both good. So is Caroline. She and Daisy are really hitting it off.

The whole picture reminds me of my imagination poster, but I don't want to leave Mr. F. I can tell he is really tired from such a big day, though I think it was a happy one for him, too.

"Mr. Fancypants likes you better now, Becket," observes Caroline on the drive home.

"True," says Nicholas, a bit sadly.

"It's because Becket takes such good care of Mr. F," says Mom. "Plus all the other farm animals."

"You certainly are proving that you can be responsible for a new pet," says Dad, with a smile at me in the rearview mirror. "What do you say to that?"

I look down at Mr. Fancypants, curled like a bagel on my lap. This whole summer, all I've wanted was a young dog like Oro to play catch and teach tricks and to make me feel like a genuine country kid.

Mr. Fancypants doesn't do any of those things. But if we got another dog, all that new-dog energy might make Mr. F feel tired, and maybe even old and left out. Besides, Mr. F is good to have around, because he's always been around. Even if I can't teach our old dog new tricks, Mr. F has probably taught me some things, like trust, loyalty, and how it takes not one but two hand-washes to get peanut butter off your skin.

"I say we already have a dog," I tell them.

In response, suddenly the car smells terrible, and everyone has to roll down the windows.

"And such a smelly dog, too!" says Caroline. "I knew Mr. F was chowing too many table scraps."

"Oh, don't you listen to her." I knuckle-rub Mr. F between his ears. "Caroline can get pretty gassy herself sometimes."

CHAPTER 19

Old Friend

MR. FANCYPANTS HAS SLEPT ON MY BED EVERY NIGHT SINCE last weekend's big thunderstorm, and this morning he wakes up a little more wheezy than usual. We're the first ones up, as I carry him downstairs. Outside, he's unsteady on his feet, but he does his business. Back inside, I give him his peanut-buttered heart pill and his breakfast, and then I put him outside again on his arthritis pillow, under his maple tree.

This morning there's just the right amount of sun and breeze, and I want him to be out in it. He coughs for a long time before he settles down.

"I'll come hang out with you later, ole boy," I tell him. Then I head to the barn to tend to Pickle and Chew. Before I go to the henhouse, I check back in with Mr. Fancypants to make sure he hasn't slurped his entire water bowl, which I'd set next to him. But he hasn't even touched it. He's in a deep, snoring sleep.

Gran is up, too. "Godiva is my total buddy now," I tell her, as I slip my hand under the hen's plump, feathered body and remove her egg. "She doesn't even cluck when she sees me." With three new chickens in the henhouse, Gran and I have collected one hundred eggs today.

"You've made all kind of friends this summer," says Gran.

"By the way, I baked a few batches of apple cider donuts early this morning to sell at the store, but why don't you come upstairs and have a couple? And then you can tell me all about Frieda's."

Now that sounds like a good morning. By the time we got home from the Franca farm last night, Gran had already gone to bed. Mostly it's Caroline who gets Gran all to herself, when Nicholas and I are at Young Explorers. So I like having some no-share time to tell Gran about the Francas, the alpacas, how glad I am to know Frieda better, and how brave I was with Suki.

"You've got a way with animals," says Gran, over warm-from-the-oven donuts. "It's in you, Becket. Patience and calm. Also, unlike a chicken, you don't ruffle easy. You've got the makings of a real farmer. I do wonder if you'll grow up to be one, like your grandfather and me."

I take another donut, and I take Gran's words to heart. It'd be fun to be a farmer one day.

When I head downstairs, Caroline is just walking into the store. "Coming up for donuts!" she calls. "Everyone wants some."

"There's plenty," calls Gran. "I'll cover a plate for you."

"You're in a good mood," I say to Caroline.

"I got a text from Daisy. She's coming over here a little later," says Caroline. "I'm going to show her around the farm. I have a hunch she'll like it better than Annabelle did."

Outside, I take a deep breath. Days feel deep-gold soft and warm with the end of summer. Mr. Fancypants hasn't moved from his pad. When I check in on him, I can sense right away that something is different.

Actually, something is wrong. I kneel down next to him, and I put my hand on the top of his head, and I feel myself go very still.

It's like all the air is stuck in my throat. I can't yell "EMERGENCY!" or "Call 911!" But I don't want to, either.

Mr. F is so still, it's like he's sleeping, the same as it's been every other summer day since we came to Blackberry Farm. But it's not. My heart is thumping so loud I can hear it in my ears. I feel body-slammed, like that time I fell off the high bars on the playground. I can't even really think about Mr. F himself. I can't even think about thinking. All I can feel is my hand, resting on Mr. Fancypants's head.

I know he is gone, but if I move my hand, it's like I have to say goodbye and I'm not quite ready to do that yet. So I stay right where I am until Gran comes outside and joins me.

"I saw you from the window," she says, sitting down next to me. Only then can I move, to hug her. Then she keeps one arm wrapped around my shoulder and squeezes me in tight. With her other hand, she gives Mr. F one last head scratch. "He was such a sweet, gentle dog."

I nod. My throat and eyes and nose feel hot and painful. Gran's shoulder turns out to be a good place for my head to rest for a while. By now, Mom and Dad and Caroline and Nicholas all have seen us from the kitchen window, and they come filing outside. Nicholas is crying pretty loud the way he does, but my feelings are somewhere deeper and more private.

The whole morning is stuck in a slow-motion haze. Gran suggests burying Mr. Fancypants under his old tree, and I nod again because Mr. F really liked it there, but also because I need some instructions. I don't have any safety tips or slogans for a pet funeral. Poor Nicholas can't stop crying. He's too upset to get Clive, and I can tell Caroline feels a little strange once Daisy is dropped off, but Daisy tells us that saying goodbye to animals is part of farm life. For the funeral, Daisy even sings a short song about a canary that flies away. It's a really pretty song about losing something you love. It also helps the rest of us get going.

Caroline is the first to speak. "Mr. Fancypants,

I always loved how you were part of the family even before I was born. You were a loving big brother, and I've known you my whole life. I'll miss you."

Caroline nudges Nicholas to talk next, but he shakes his head. He's been crying so hard, he just can't.

Mom looks at me. "Do you have anything to say, Becket?"

As it turns out, I do. "Mr. Fancypants, the main

thing that you accomplished was your amazing oldness. We were lucky to know you for so long," I say. "Tomorrow, I won't see you enjoy the sun on your face. I won't give you your peanut butter pills. I won't get to scratch behind your ears while you settle in for a nap. Not getting to share your day with you, Mr. Fancypants, will be the worst part about tomorrow."

I spend the rest of my day outside, walking and looking for Beautiful Alerts. In the afternoon, Caroline invites Nicholas and me into her room. We flip through family photo albums and then we play Pictionary until Dad calls us down for dinner. I'd brought Mr. F's special cushion back inside earlier, but I can't even look at it.

After dinner, I go up to bed. I get out my Country Kid List to look at the excellent portrait of Mr. Fancypants I'd drawn on the bottom of it earlier this summer.

I'm still holding it later when Mom, Dad, and Gran all come to tuck me in.

"You know Mr. F wasn't doing well for a while," says Gran. "His heart had been failing for some time."

I nod. I knew that.

"You watched him more carefully than anyone, Becket," says Mom. "You must have noticed that he'd been having trouble breathing. How confused he'd become. Even with his pills to help, he was fading."

I nod again. "Knowing didn't make it easier."

"No, of course not. A vet's eye is different from a family's heart. But you have both. You'd make a great vet one day." She glances over at my list and sees my drawing. "Gosh, or an artist. You really captured him. Oh, is this your Country Kid List?"

"Yep," I say. "I'd probably have just chucked this list when I started school. But now with my Mr. F drawing on it, I never will."

"It's a good way to remember your summer *and*

Mr. F, who ended up being a big part of it," says Dad. "I think you should put that list somewhere for safekeeping, Becket."

"Hey, you just called me by my new name for the very first time."

"Really?" Dad looks puzzled. Then his eyes crinkle. "I hadn't realized. Maybe I needed some time to grow into it."

Mom rereads my list. "Was this the summer you thought it would be?"

I shake my head. "In the beginning, I figured if I did ten things that I hadn't ever done, it would make me into a real country kid. But this summer didn't follow my list. I never knew what I needed to learn next." I pull up my covers and put some penguins on me. "I still don't."

"That's life," says Gran. "Most reliable thing about it are the twists and turns."

After everyone says good night, and the light is out, and I'm alone, I stay awake in the moonlit dark. Even though Mr. F only slept on the edge of my bed for his last days, I miss the lump of him.

Eventually I slip downstairs and bring up his arthritis cushion from the kitchen. I put it under my window so that the moonlight hits it. It doesn't make me cry, after all. It helps me to see him in my mind.

And when I listen to the sounds of the pond frogs, I can almost hear him snoring still.

"Good night, ole boy," I whisper.

HOW TO BE
A COUNTRY KID

1. Goodbye, City!
2. Change My Name **to Becket**
3. Do Barnyard Chores ~~(to Get a Country Dog)~~ **and Learn How to Care for Animals**
4. Make a New ~~Best~~ Friend
5. **Get Rich Quick (and Pay My Debts)**
6. Drive a Tractor (Like a Natural)!!!
7. Make Something Special
8. Survive a Brush with Danger
9. Host the Fairs **(in Rain and Shine)**
10. ~~Visit~~ **Catch** an Alpaca ~~Farm~~
11. Be a Friend Till the End

Acknowledgments

From the moment my daughter picked the head off a dandelion and tucked it behind her ear with a gleeful "Beautiful Alert!" this book found both its catchphrase and its value. Thank you, Priscilla, for the nature-loving exuberance that inspired Becket.

To Team Algonquin, you are my other Beautiful Alert. What a pleasure to have every detail of this book so carefully considered. With extra helpings of heartfelt thanks to my editor, Elise Howard, for our painstaking work through our own lists of "How to Make a Becket Book."

I always love to give a shout-out to my first readers and early true Becket cheering team, Emily van Beek and Courtney Sheinmel. Your reads are my confidence-boosting energy drink!

Another shout from the rooftop to the incredible LeUyen Pham, for injecting such imaginative life and humor into the whole Blackberry Farm family. What a thrill for Becket and me.

Finally, a big hug to Erin Dockery, DVM, for her knowledgeable, compassionate care of our dog, Edith, through her twilight years. We are a lucky family, both human and animal, to have such a wonderful neighborhood vet and friend.